Rescuing Clarice

Victoria Morton

Published by Trellis Publishing, 2021.

This is a work of fiction. Similarities to real people, places, or events are entirely coincidental.

RESCUING CLARICE

First edition. July 11, 2021.

Copyright © 2021 Victoria Morton.

ISBN: 979-8224827169

Written by Victoria Morton.

RESCUING CLARICE
VICTORIA MORTON

RESCUING CLARICE

The tears came down this time in torrents, not as soft and partially concealed as it used to but in hot salty torrents. It felt so real and vivid. Living the memories every night felt like a curse. Her pillows were yet again soaked with tears as she struggled on her bed while the gruff Indian stripped her like they always took turns to every night. She was their slave and their entertainment. Some nights she fed just one, other nights she fed two, three or more of them with the sweet nectar between her thighs; the nectar she had jealously guarded since she understood what violating it could do to her person. Clarice struggled until all she could do was trash against the bed she was tied to and cry until the Indian felt he had had enough of her for the night.

"You should save those tears for the trashing. Your old man wronged the wrong people." The Indian leader who was stuffing his mouth with meat said. They had taken her to their hideout deep in the woods where noblemen dared not go. The Indians had ravaged the town of Wyoming and terrorized every nook and cranny of the city. The businesses which were still up and running in Wyoming have since settled the Indians to stay in business. Business owners who couldn't, closed down theirs or moved to a safer town but Clarice's father; Marc Grayling had threatened the Indians with the Sheriff, little did he know that the Sheriff was in on the bounties the Indians brought home. Clarice Grayling had watched her parents and brother as they squirted out blood from their mouths while the Indians drove knives continuously into their bodies. Their death was a gruesome one and watching them die like chickens had been the beginning of her trauma.

Clarice awoke to the deafening silence of the woods while the nightmare she had just had haunted her sanity. She had given up on escaping as the town's Sheriff had once caught her running away from her captors and returned her to them. She hated the Sheriff and everyone who worked with the Indians. Clarice listened but heard nothing. The room was too dark for her to see anything and she was still bound to a loosely-tied rope. That was awkward, but her head began to spin another escape plan. She didn't care where they had gone to but she knew they would be back and she had to be gone before they were back. She worked her teeth against her binds determined to get her hands out of it. The sudden firing of gunshots caused her to freeze. It stopped after a while, and it dawned on her that the Indians were either being raided or were raiding an unsuspecting merchant. She eased herself up and against the hardwood of the bed and continued working on the binds until they snapped. Tiptoeing across the creaking floorboards, she made it outside, but the scene her eyes met with was an unexpected one. Lying before her and murdered in cold blood were the Indians that had held her captive for years.

She could still hear the shots being fired, but she wasn't going to stand there and wait to see who it was. Clarice tore into the woods running as fast as her legs could take her. Her feet trashed upon dried leaves and twigs which cut her, but she pushed on.

All of a sudden a ray of light blinded her, and she ran headfirst into the strongest chest she had ever come in contact with.

"Hey Missy, you have to be still," the owner of the chest said with a husky voice she thought was sexy. "Let go of me," she screamed, kicking. His strong hands clamped over her mouth preventing her from saying more words.

"I'm trying to help you here, Missy. If those Indians get a hold of you again, I'll definitely not come back to get you out," Clarice tried to reply, but her words were muffled.

"Fine! I'll let you speak, but you must promise not to scream once I let go," Clarice nodded unsure why he was whispering. Gradually he uncovered her mouth, and she spun around to get a better view of his face. He was carefully decked out in his Sheriff attire and looked younger than the previous Sheriffs the town had had.

"Oh, the sheriff comes to my rescue. I should be so glad," she said rolling her eyes while walking away from him. "What are you going to do, send me back right? I'll save you the stress and go back to them than have you deliver me like pizza."

"Wait, have you gone insane? Nobody said anything about taking you back. If you want to get out of here, you should follow me right now before dawn meets us here." the Sheriff said.

"And why should I trust you?" she asked hands folded across her chest. "Look around you Ma'am, have you any other choice?" he asked.

"I guess not," she said and stomped after him. She wasn't sure where he was taking her, but she sensed something sincere and different about him. A few minutes later they stepped out into a clearing where the sheriff's car was hidden by the surrounding trees, and grasses. She shivered from the cold and her teeth chattered.

"Here, have my jacket," he said pulling his jacket to reveal a white t-shirt beneath.

"Thank you so much Sheriff; you are quite different from the others,"

"Call me Colin, please," the sheriff said with a smile.

"Why do you keep saying that? Did you have such bad experiences with the previous sheriffs of this town?" he asked as he guided her to the passenger's side of the car. "It's an experience I'd rather not tell; please get me far away from here.

"Would you like to come home with me, that is if you don't have any other place to go?" Colin asked. Clarice thought of her home. It must have been overgrown with weeds and probably buried in dust. She had always dreamed of a life of happiness with her loving family, but the Indians had taken that dream away from her. "I wouldn't want to be a bother, but I promise to leave once I can find where to go. She had no other relative in Wyoming, and the Sheriff has already proven that he could be trusted.

"You don't have to be in a hurry to leave. You should take a good look at yourself, you need some time to recover and someone to take care of you," he said shutting the door after her. The air about him was friendly, and she suddenly wanted to know more about him and why he was helping her escape.

"You never told me your name?" Colin said as he revved the car's engine to life and drove off.

"Oh, I'm Clarice Grayling." She sounded polite and friendly but there was a certain resentment in her voice that he knew would take time to leave.

Colin's ranch was aglow with beautiful lights. It was the biggest ranch she had seen, and it reminded her of her home. She knew she could never be normal again after the terrible ordeal she had undergone in the hands of the Indians. She felt like damaged goods and blamed herself for being a female and a beautiful one when she was captured. She felt hopeless and wondered why Colin was helping her. He's probably doing this because he knows how helpless and hopeless my situation is, she thought as a tear crawled down her right cheek. Her skin made her cringe, and she wished she could take a vacation from her skin away from the nightmares that haunted her every time she shut her eyes.

"We are here," Colin said as he put off the engine and stepped out of the car. You're welcome to my ranch. Make yourself at home."

"Thank you," she said as she walked into the room beside his. Clarice wondered about the room which was carefully organized as if in anticipation of her arrival.

"It's a beautiful place you have here," Clarice said as she noticed he was standing at the door. "Thank you," he said as a smile cracked open his mouth. Colin felt a wave of satisfaction wash over him as he headed towards his room. He would call in his doctor tomorrow and make sure he took good care of Clarice as he wouldn't want her to fall ill from all she had undergone.

***

For the first time in a long time Clarice woke up feeling refreshed and liberated. She had not screamed or felt the ropes bite into her wrists as she struggled to clear the memories of her gory past while being fed more demons every night. She was awake and in a bed whose quilt scented like fresh lilies. She could hear horse hooves and it calmed her nerves. Life felt promising but what could be promising about being damaged. Her body ached as she sat up to look out of the window above her head. Summer's fresh air hit her nostrils, and she inhaled deeply.

"Hi. Up already? Early riser huh?" Colin asked popping his head into her room. His voice caught her off guard causing her to fall into her bed. Colin threw back his head and laughed heartily. He had never laughed so hard in a long time. Clarice sat up to get a better view of the handsome sheriff who had helped her escape the night before. She had so many questions to ask him, but surprisingly all she could get out was a 'Hi'. She stared at his hairy chest and strong arms. The sun rays filtering into the room through the window cast a glow on his skin causing his features to gleam. The sweat that ran down his abs stirred up something in her, but she cautioned herself to behave.

"Do you like what you see or would you prefer I put some clothes on?" Colin asked with a mischievous grin. "Put on some clothes please," she said gently tearing her eyes away. She was not supposed to be attracted to him, not after everything that has happened to her. She took every attraction she could feel and wrapped it up and shoving it down her heart where she felt no emotion could survive; she reached for a shawl and wrapped it around her body. His reaction after that action baffled her.

"Put that right back and never touch anything in this room again. As a matter of fact, this farm has an empty cottage not far from this one. You can stay there while you work for me. All you have to do is take care of my home, and I'll pay you at the end of every week," he said.

"I'm sorry if I angered you Mr. Colin, but you don't have to be a jackass about it, it's just a shawl."

"What do you know anyway," he said taking the shawl from her and placing it neatly in the drawer she had taken it from.

"I'll have a friend deliver some clothes you can use while you work here and I'll have a doctor ascertain that you're fit to work before you start."

"Alright Sheriff, I'll leave before you are back from work. She said with her head bowed. Colin felt a sudden surge of remorse. The shawl meant a lot to him, but it wasn't her fault that she didn't know it did. It had belonged to his late wife who had died in the hands of Indians long before he moved to Wyoming.

"What happened to the Indians anyway? Was it your team that attacked them or were they attacked by a rival group? How did you even find me?" Clarice who saw the remorse written on his face asked.

Colin checked his watch to know if he had enough time to answer her questions. When he saw that he had some time to clear the air, he plopped down on the fluffy quilt and started with an apology.

"I'm sorry I replied you in that manner. You didn't deserve that. I let my emotions get a better hold of me." He paused and looked down at his hand for some time before looking up at her. She looked so tired and beautiful like she had always been.

"That shawl belonged to my late wife, Gretchen but that..." he said raising his index finger in a hush manner in order to keep the questions he saw in her eyes at bay, "... is a story I can only tell you when you tell me how you got roped in with the Indians. He watched her reactions and saw that she cringed at the mention of the word 'Indians'.

"Oh, I guess that would take a long while then," she said wrapping the bed covering around her. How had she slept in that revealing nightwear? She wondered. Had he taken off her clothes in the night?"

she had slept like a log and so hadn't noticed any movement in the room the whole night.

"I had a worker change you up last night. I wouldn't have done that myself," he replied. She heaved a sigh as her facial features relaxed. Colin choked up a smile and proceeded with the information she had asked of him.

"I was out riding on my first night as a Sheriff to this town. I had been asked to assist the previous Sheriff as he was under scrutiny. He had shady deals with the Indians, but he was smart enough to cover his tracks. So while I was out with Mario, we stopped by a river in the woods which was just by a little cottage to have a drink."

"Mario? Is that like your colleague or something?" Clarice asked with raised eyebrows.

"Mario is my late wife's favorite horse. I was wondering what life would have been like if she was around to tour the new town with me, so I took her horse for a ride."

"Oh, I understand now," Clarice said and waited for him to continue.

"While Mario drank from the river, I decided to check out the cottage. I realized after my tour that it had been used as a hideout and it made me wander deep into the woods with Mario, and that was how I found you. You were tied up in a makeshift cage while some Indians threw food at you like they would a dog." He paused as if to gauge the effect of his words on the girl who sat with his back to him, a girl who unknown to him was being mentally tortured by every word he said.

"You were much younger then and reminded me so much of my sister. I couldn't trust anybody in the system then because I didn't know who was loyal to the sheriff, so I kept quiet about what I had found out.

"I was just an assistant who didn't know much about the town he had been shipped to anyway so you wouldn't blame me for not speaking up. I had to make sure the Sheriff was not in on any of it..."

"But he was in all of it. He even sent me back one of the times he caught me escaping. That was why I thought you'd do the same thing." Clarice said cutting him off.

"I'm sorry about that Clarice, I really am. I tried to get the FBI to see that he was apprehended, but I got a threat that said I would be relocated if I kept sticking my nose in their affairs. I was the only hope you had for an escape, so I laid low while I planned the clash of yesternight. I had some good townsmen who had become friends with me stage an attack which I and some trusted FBI agents prepared them for. The preparation kicked off after they were sure the former sheriff was of no good to this town."

"Oh, I guess it took a really long while for the good fishes to see who the shark really was huh? And now, where are they?"

"They? Who?"

"The Indians who assaulted me every night and left me broken?" she said with a raised voice.

"All dead. They died in the shootout last night. It had just been a plan to get them behind bars, but they'd rather fight." Colin said.

Clarice broke into tears. "Does it really matter that they are dead? Their death doesn't change how damaged I've become. It doesn't repair my broken heart, and it doesn't make me resent men less. It doesn't take away my nightmares, and it definitely won't bring back my family," she said with all the hurt she could muster. Picking up a robe she had seen hanging in the wardrobe, she started for the door but stopped in her tracks.

"Thank you for finally living up to what we revere Sheriffs for, but you were not in time to save me from the derogatory life I had been put through. Now I get to live with the nightmares, not you, not anyone, Me!" She said and stomped off towards the cottage set strategically aside from that of the workers he had on his farm. Just as he had described, it was small, but it was just right for her and everything she felt at that moment. It smelled of dust, and cobwebs lined the walls of the house. It had only one room which was big enough to accommodate two people. It must have been some sort of a lover's nest, and she wondered how many women he had had on the bed that invited her to lay in it. She pushed the thoughts away from her mind and set about making the little cottage her new home.

Later that afternoon, a lady came knocking with the list of her work on the farm. According to what Colin had written, she was to take care of the house he lived in, feed Mario and Spark when he wasn't around. He trusted her enough to let her handle the horses which mattered to him. The others were going to be taken care of by his other workers. She was to supervise their work whenever he was not around to do so.

"That's quite a lot to be handled by me," she said with a sigh but work, she must. She couldn't bear the shame of living for free in a man's house — a man who wasn't her husband. Clarice set about the day's job cleaning and cleaning until Colin's house was sparkling like diamonds. She got curious sometimes and went through some of his pictures, but she found nothing suspicious. She went out into the farm to check on the workers. They didn't like her presence, but they acted as though they wanted her around forever. Clarice was able to ignore the talks that flew behind her back on some days and on other days; she would run to her cottage and cry her eyes out. Their distaste for her and the fact that she had been with the Indians almost all her life was clearly written in the eyes of every male and female she walked past while in town. The small-town gossip was centered on her and on the sheriff who picked up a whore for his pleasure.

Although it wasn't the truth, but that was typical town gossip; most of them held no water. Some of the ruthless townsfolk threw rotten food at her whenever she stopped at their stores to buy their goods, while wayward men leered at her and spanked her butt most times inviting her to bed with them.

One of the ladies who gathered hay for the men to tie up in bundles had a little girl with her who loved showing Clarice around the farm whenever she came for supervision. The first day she met Leila's mother, she was cleaning out the stables, and her daughter was feeding the horses whose stables were already cleaned out.

"Hello Ma'am, I'm Clarice Grayling," She stuck out her hand from the back of her dress where she always had it and waited for a handshake.

"Please don't be like the others, please don't be like the others," she muttered under her breath. She had not been able to find a friend amongst the other workers, and it was beginning to get her depressed.

"I can hear you, Clarice and I'm not like the others," she replied with a smile and took off her gloves to give her a handshake. "I am Kate Evans, Colin's sister," the woman said. Clarice stood dumbfounded unable to articulate her next words.

"I'm really sorry Ma'am, I really didn't know you were and oh, who is the adorable young lady with you?" she asked as Leila ran to meet her mother for more apples.

"She's my daughter, Leila."

"Oh Hey Leila, it's nice to meet you. I'm Clarice and I'm new to the farm. I can see you're having a great time with the horses." Clarice said with the brightest smile she could offer the little girl. She didn't want the little girl to see her as the unfriendly one. Having a kid's bright smile each day could help her get through her day, and this was her chance of making Leila her best friend on the farm.

"Hi Clarice, come help me feed the horses with more apples," the little girl said dragging her towards the horses. After that day, Leila became the only one who she looked forward to seeing every day.

***

Colin loved riding into the mountains nearby, every weekend. He used to do that with his wife when she was around. These days the morning rides were no longer interesting, and he didn't look forward to them like before. He walked into the stable and right into Clarice who was heading out of the stable with Mario.

"Where are you taking him to?" Colin asked surprised she could handle Mario.

"For a little run in the fields. I figured it wouldn't be so bad since you do not take him out for rides anymore." Colin dimmed his eyes as if in suspicion that she had been spying on him.

"Have you been spying on me?"

"I wouldn't call it spying. I've literally been held hostage for a long while. I saw the picture you took on one of the mountains in the far west. I had to piece the puzzle together." Clarice said.

"Let's go for a ride. That is if you can comfortably sit on him without being thrown over." Colin said as he went for Spark. The black thoroughbred brushed his face against his.

"I've missed you too, Spark. Ready for a ride?" Spark neighed in response. Let's do this then," he said as he got on the black horse and headed out of the stables.

He was surprised when he saw Mario behind with Clarice atop him. "Wow," he exclaimed giving her that look that said he respected her for working whatever magic she did with Mario.

"How did you get him to do that? He never lets anyone sit on him except me and of course Gretchen."

Clarice smiled as she willed the horse to keep moving. "A Cowgirl never lets her secrets out."

"Oh well, we are about to see that happen," he said, "Hiyaa!" he shouted as spark took off on the path towards the mountains.

"C'mon Mario we are not about to let him rub his ego on our faces. Go! Go! Go!" She yelled at the horse who took off at top speed leaving dust on one of the ranch workers who stood and watched them in a bid to gather more things to gossip about.

"Take that nitwit. Next time you stick your nose in your own batter." She screamed and laughed out loud. She had not ridden a horse in a long while, and it felt refreshing having the summer wind in her face and hair. Before long, Colin and Clarice were galloping side by side and taunting each other's tactics. Colin felt alive again. Looking at her face and the beautiful smile which made her eyes glow, he felt that stir in his stomach again. He had made sure to avoid her all these days that she had been on the same farm with him but how much longer would he continue to act like he didn't wake up early every morning to watch her clean and eat breakfast before he left the house.

Colin stood on the mountain and staring out into the valley; nostalgia hit him. He doubled over from the effect it had on his heart, and he began to panic. Clarice rushed over to his side and lifted his head to rest on her laps while she spoke words reassuring him that everything would be fine.

"Here have some water, you will be alright," Clarice said as she brought a bottle of water she had stashed away in her leather bag to his mouth. Colin inhaled deeply after gulping down mouthfuls of water. He sat up as his breathing normalized.

"Thank you, Clarice," he said with a sad smile and turned away. The air was charged with emotion that seemed to rip them apart gently from the inside.

"My father refused to be in business with the Indians," Clarice began after a moment's silence. She wiped at the tears that fell from her eyes in a way that Colin wouldn't notice she was crying. "The very day they visited my home, they took everything I had with them."

"How do you mean everything?" Colin whose eyes were still lost in the distance asked.

"They killed my parents and my only brother, and after making me watch them die slowly, they took me, hostage. Every day they trashed me for my father's refusal to give them what they wanted and every night they violated me," she held back the emotions that wracked through her body like electric sparks as she didn't want pity from the Sheriff who had cared enough to break the jinx.

"That's the cruelest thing I've ever heard. And the sheriffs, they did nothing?" Colin asked turning to get a better look at her. His heart broke into different shards when he caught sight of her glassy eyes. She couldn't let the tears fall anymore; she was done crying for her damaged self.

"They were afraid of them. Some dined and clinked glasses of wine with them while others hid in their offices acting like the Indians didn't exist. No day passed by that I didn't wish that I joined my family that night but I couldn't because I was tied to the bed; I couldn't even take my own life," she said hitting her chest for emphasis. "I willed death to take me, but it seemed not to pay heed to my wishes. I even tried escaping once but was caught by the sheriff who returned me to the Indians instead of taking me far away from them. Then you came along and here we are today," she concluded.

Colin drew her into his arms and wiped her tears. He knew firsthand what it was like to feel like damaged goods and how worthless any lady who had undergone what she had been through should feel.

"My sister was taken hostage by bandits too and violated. She was released when they found out she was pregnant and they went on their merry way leaving her to die by a river. A kind-hearted fellow found her and brought her back to me. Leila is the result of that pregnancy," he said with a weak smile. Colin opened his mouth allowing air that flowed in to calm his soul before he continued. "I fought day and night trying to keep her from taking her life and that of her child. So believe me, Clarice, when I say that I know exactly how you feel," Colin said. His eyes lingered on her mouth and strayed upwards to her eyes. She saw the hunger in his eyes and decided to give in to what her heart wanted. She let her dress slip revealing her flawless bare shoulders. It was his cue, but he knew he couldn't take it.

"I want you as much as you want me and you can have me here and now," Clarice said stretching out seductively and taunting the handsome sheriff before her. His blood pressure fired up as his heart raced. She looked as beautiful as ever, and he wanted everything she was offering him.

"No, I can't have you in this state," Colin said pulling away from her.

"I figured, who wants damaged goods anyway," she said with exasperation as she pulled up her dress and dusted her boots.

"Don't ever say that," Colin said turning towards her and holding her cheeks tenderly. She felt so fragile and he feared he might break her. "I can't have you in your vulnerable state. You might hate me afterward, and that is not what I want from a woman I lo.." he began and paused when he realized what he had almost said.

"A woman you love? You love me?" Clarice queried her eyes begging for answers.

"Yes, Clarice," he said holding her gaze. She loved him too he could see the emotions swirling in her eyes. His mouth no longer needed an invitation as it found its way to hers and before long they both were curled into each other making memories they'd forever cherish.

***

The fire started in the barns. Nobody seemed to know how but it looked like a deliberate act to bring down the farm than a mistake. The horses took off in different directions as the flames crept towards the stables; by morning half of the farm had burnt down. A search was conducted to know where the fire could have started from when a worker stumbled on a familiar hat which belonged to the only female who had access to the barns and to the account section of the farmhouse; Clarice.

Gretchen walked into Colin's room feeling betrayed. I told you she was of no good; now she didn't just lose half of what you owned while gambling her life away with those swindlers at the inn, she also felt it convenient to kill us all why we slept at night.

Clarice who didn't know why firefighters were at the barn and why Gretchen was shouting at Colin walked in reeking of alcohol. She had since taken to that lifestyle after she overheard Colin telling his sister that whatever had happened between at the mountains had been a mistake. She felt worthless and betrayed. Colin had broken her heart with those words, and she was bent on living life like it no longer mattered. She had gotten drunk a week after at the inn and had given away half of what Colin owned to cheating gamblers while he was away with his sister. Colin had let her off with a warning but the hurt and rage that burned within him this time wanted to see her behind bars. She had betrayed the love he had for her by attempting to roast him while he slept.

"You coward!" Gretchen spat and walked away when she staggered into his room.

"Hey, why's your sister behaving funny and why do you have my hat? Hand it over will you please," she said extending her hands.

"You are not even sorry for what you've done?" Colin's voice rose above normal. He never raised his voice on her, but this incident didn't call for calm talks.

"Who made you do this? Who put you up to it?" He asked.

"Do what? And please you are being too loud, I have a headache already," Clarice said holding her head unable to understand why the sheriff was yelling.

"Why did you try to burn the farm down? I loved you Clarice, and all you did was try to burn down my farm?"

"We are still standing here, so your farm wasn't burnt down. Anyway, I didn't do it, and I pray you find out who did." Her words lacked emotion, and he wondered what had changed since their ecstatic moment at the mountain.

"If you claim that you had nothing to do with the fire, then what was your hat doing seated in the scene of the fire?"

"I don't know how my hat got there, but you can rest assured that I had nothing to do with the fire," she said.

"Liar!" He yelled his eyes spitting hot stares that could raze down a farm.

"You're the liar here Mr. Sheriff. Telling me that you loved me and turning back and saying what we had was a mistake? Now I sincerely wish that I set that fire. I hate you!" She yelled and took off in the direction of her little cottage. She knew she had to leave, but it had to be when she could feel her feet. She plopped onto her bed and cried herself to sleep.

Colin's anger was suddenly doused when she let him know she had overheard the conversation he had had with her sister. He loved her with all his heart, but he was scared of what his sister would think of him loving someone who had been with the Indians, the same ones who had nearly damaged her life. He had told her that her sister had been attacked by bandits instead as he didn't want her to think he was with her because she reminded him of his sister's ordeal. He walked towards the barn for the second time that evening puzzled. He couldn't believe he had crashed his one chance at love and that he couldn't identify who would set Clarice up. Just then he noticed an awkward movement behind the stables close to the barn. He tiptoed close enough to listen on the conversation but whoever was behind the stables had stopped talking. It was getting dark, and he could only make out the silhouette of the person cast against the wall by the flickering bulb behind the stables; whoever it was had his back to him and was working on the cables that brought in light to the stables. That was it.

The cables of the barn's lighting had been tampered with as well, causing the fire the night before. He tiptoed towards him and knocked the intruder down with his gun. It turned out to be one of the workers in the barn. Clarice had often complained about him saying that he hated her and detested the fact she was made supervisor instead of him. Colin dragged him into the stables and chained him to a pole. He would be out till the next morning as he had taken the hit to the head.

He double checked his chains to make sure that even if he woke up while everybody slept, he wouldn't be able to free himself of the binds.

Colin paced his room unable to figure out the best way to win Clarice back. He didn't care what his sister had to say or what the townsfolk had to say anymore. He loved her, and that was what mattered.

"What are you doing wearing holes into that poor carpet?" Gretchen asked when she walked in on a pacing Colin.

"You were wrong. We were both wrong, and we have to apologize to her first thing tomorrow morning. I can't lose her too. I love, and I care about you. But if you love me as much as you've made me understand then you'll be fine with my decisions Gretch," Colin pelted out in a rush.

"You are making no sense. Who did we wrong and what decisions are you talking about?" a confused Gretchen asked.

"Clarice was set up by one of the workers. I caught him out behind the stables some minutes ago tampering with the electric cables wired to the stables. I have him tied up, and he will be taken to the station where he'll be charged with arson." Gretchen stared at his brother dumbfounded. Suddenly they heard horse hooves, and when he looked out the window, he saw a carriage in front of Clarice's little cottage.

"She's leaving; I can't let her leave. Gretchen, please help me," he said and ran out towards the cottage that housed the love of his life while his sister and little Leila who had been eavesdropping followed behind him.

"Clarice please don't leave. I'm sorry. I just didn't know what to think with your behavior and the hat found at the barn, but I caught one of the workers who I suspect had set you up. I'm very sorry I hurt you. Please don't go," Colin pleaded, holding onto her hand. Clarice knew she loved him, but she doubted if she could trust him.

"This was a mistake, remember? Why do you want me to stay and keep making mistakes?" Clarice asked looking away from him so that she could have the courage to walk away when the time came. But that time never came because Gretchen apologized and got Leila to beg on their behalf. Clarice loved Leila and couldn't deny her anything. Moreover, she was still in love with her handsome sheriff, and if it would take a second chance to find out if she really was cut out for love, then she would jump on her horse to take it.

Looking into the eyes of the handsome man who some months ago had risked his life to save her from her tormentors, she knew he was worth all the chances he asked for. If he could walk right into danger, then I can walk over his mistakes and love him as I've always wanted to, she thought and disregarding Gretchen and Leila's presence, Clarice covered his lips with hers in want, and drawing him into her cottage, she drew him into her life forever.

THE END...

THE BEAUTIFUL CHOICE

ERICA FANNING

Jeremiah Schwartz was deeply in love with this wonderful woman, named Rachel Miller. Rachel was a beautiful woman, with long brown hair and big brown eyes to match. She was the sweetest woman you could ever meet and was never rude to anyone in authority. She always followed the rules and made sure her friends did the same.

One day, during the time of Rumspringa, *on a beautiful Sunday evening, Jeremiah and his friends had been drinking—experimenting really—and had started to get a little rowdier than usual. Rachel approached Jeremiah about this and told him he needed to stop drinking if he was ever going to have a chance with her, because she knew that was the only way to get him to stop.*

"Ah, it's only a little liquor," he said defiantly as he took another swig. His friends laughed and cheered as Rachel blushed and hurried to leave.

Daniel King, the young man who had just been voted to be the next preacher of the town saw all of this happen. He also loved Rachel very much and, instead of correcting the boys on their behavior as his duty was, he went after the maiden since they were already secretly dating and had begun planning their wedding in secret.

As Daniel ran out, Jeremiah saw him go. There was no way anyone was going to take his beautiful brown eyed girl from him. For no matter how foolish he had been, he was going to make things right. In a flash, he left his friends for his love. By the time he reached the door, he could tell he was already too late. Daniel was already leading Rachel to his carriage to take her home.

"Hey!"

The pair stopped and turned as the intoxicated man came toward them, nostrils flaring. He bunched up his fists ready for a fight, and Daniel saw as much. In a gesture of bravery, he stepped in between the girl and Jeremiah, ready to defend her if need be. The next few moments happened very quickly, and before either man or Rachel knew what happened, there was an unconscious man on the ground... and it wasn't Daniel. Without thinking, Daniel began punching the unconscious man in a sudden rage of fury he didn't even know he had in him. No one was going to take his bride-to-be from him that easily. He kept punching and punching and punching. In the back of his mind he heard Rachel screaming. Heard himself screaming. There was blood everywhere, on him, on his clothes, even on Rachel.

"Hey man, wake up!"

Daniel woke with start and pushed himself up, ready to strike.

"Whoa, dude! You seriously need to look into an Amish psychiatrist or something." It was Daniel's cellmate, Robert Meyers, who preferred to be called Bobby. Daniel put his hands down and apologized. "Dude, you were seriously screaming. Like, I don't know what was going on, but it seriously sounded like you needed an exorcist or something."

Bobby loved to use the word "seriously" as if the word would suddenly be gone if he didn't use it at least once in a sentence. It was better than what most of the other inmates said on a regular basis, so Daniel never made a big deal about it.

"Sometimes I feel like I need an exorcist, Bobby. I don't understand how anyone can kill someone else... especially more than one person." Bobby nodded, understanding.

"Still having nightmares?" Daniel nodded. These "nightmares" were really just a reenactment of the night he killed Jeremiah Schwartz, and they were always from different perspectives. Maybe it was from hearing all of the different viewpoints in court, or maybe it was just a curse that God had placed on him so that he would never forget about that night.

Daniel King had been sentenced to 10 years in prison for voluntary manslaughter, however, he had been such a good inmate that the judge was letting him out after only 1 year... on the condition that he see a parole officer for the duration of the sentence. Today was his release day, and seeing the parole officer was a small price to pay for the large debt he created in his life and the lives of those closest to him and to Jeremiah.

At one point in time, Daniel and Jeremiah had been nearly inseparable. Growing up, they were never far from each other and were always the pranksters of the class. Rachel had been the only one to keep them from getting into real trouble most of the time as she had always had that way with people that caused children to stay out of trouble even when they should have been. Daniel smiled sadly to himself as he remembered the good times with his two friends... and now one of them was dead and the other one probably wished he was. Bobby saw the look in his eyes.

"Hey, you can't do that to yourself again, Mr. Internalizer. You're seriously getting out today! That's like, the best thing ever! I've seriously got another 20 years. So be happy you're getting out after ONE. That's seriously amazing!" Daniel looked at his friend and smiled. He shook his head.

"I can't believe you sometimes." Bobby furrowed his brow slightly.

"What do you mean? What did I do?"

"You're always so happy. You're in prison, but you're literally one of the happiest people I've ever met." Daniel was sure not to use "seriously"... sometimes that only made it worse.

Bobby flashed his goofy grin and answered, "I've already told you my secret, man. Religion will change you if you let it."

Daniel scoffed. "Please don't give me that religion spiel. I tried religion, I grew up in it. That's all that being Amish is: religion."

Bobby laughed before correcting himself, "I used 'religion', but what I have isn't just religion, it's more like a relationship. And sure, it's with the same God that you claim to serve, but it's seriously different. Because I get to learn his heart for people, and not just his 'rules.' I bet if you really gave him a chance, he would change your whole perspective on life... and you would seriously quit beating yourself up about..." Bobby paused, deciding if he wanted to finish with the sentence Daniel was sure was about to be a pun. "Well, about seriously beating a guy to death." And there it was. Daniel shook his head. He wasn't sure he really wanted to try a relationship with the same Creator he had learned all his life was angry and distant.

"I don't know, man," Daniel finally conceded. Maybe when I'm feeling down, I'll just write you so you can write me an encouraging word for the week." Daniel winked as the realization hit Bobby that his friend was being sarcastic.

"Hey, you better write to me anyway," Bobby said threateningly as if he could do anything about it. "I'll seriously cry if you don't."

"No you won't."

"Yeah I will. And don't tell me otherwise. Seriously."

Daniel laughed. "Help me pack... seriously."

Over the last year, Bobby had learned a lot about Daniel and his life as a Plain man. There was one thing that few people knew however, and even Bobby was surprised when he found out; Daniel and Rachel were not only engaged, but were to be secretly married the following day. Although many of the Plain youths had to be at court to testify, Rachel never made eye contact with Daniel, not even when asked to look at him by Daniel's attorney. It cut Daniel to the heart that the one true love of his life wanted nothing to do with him.

Daniel had begun to wonder over the last year if going back was even worth it, but he had learned one thing from Bobby: squeeze the day. That basically meant that no matter what happens, just go for it and get every bit of enjoyment or pain or whatever else may come that you can out of the moment. In a "safe" environment like the penitentiary, it was easy practice, but it was also a very structured environment. You can only get away with and do so much before you have to stop.

As Daniel was driven to the edge of his community, he determined he was simply going to squeeze the day, no matter what. It had been almost two years since he'd been in his community or even laid eyes on it. He had been taken by police that night since Jeremiah's younger brother had been secretly keeping a cell phone on him at all times. He was the one to call the police, and he was the reason Daniel felt the worst about what happened. Although Jeremiah wasn't super responsible, he was the main caretaker of his family. Killing him meant that his younger brother Josiah had to take over, and he was only 14 at the time. There were three other siblings in the family after Josiah. The youngest one, Jovienne, had just turned 3.

After Jovienne was born, the Schwartz's mother had died from cancer and the father drank himself to death within weeks from trying to numb the pain of losing the love of his life. The community had done their best to find any relatives to care for the Schwartz children, but there was no one. So Jeremiah had been charged with being the head of household while the community did what they could to pitch in. After his father passed, Jeremiah was never the same. Since he was nearly 16, the age to start dating, he experimented a bit with alcohol as well with some of the other rowdy boys. Daniel and Rachel tried to get him away from the friends and the alcohol as much as possible since they knew it had already destroyed Jeremiah's father. Eventually, Jeremiah stopped listening to his true friends altogether and became something like the town drunk on Sunday evenings. Around the same time, Daniel and Rachel started courting without Jeremiah's knowledge. Rachel had wanted to tell Jeremiah to avoid too much conflict and because he was their friend, but Daniel didn't want any kind of confrontation. Everyday he wished he would have been the friend that Jeremiah needed, but the past was the past and he was back to squeeze the day.

While his mind had been floundering on the past, he eventually found his physical form had fixed itself on the doorstep of the Miller residence. He knew that he had to see Rachel before going into town. The last time he checked, she had always had that gift of quelling any argument and Daniel knew if he had her on his side, the community would be more willing to accept him. Tentatively, he knocked on the door. In a quick moment, the door flung open and Isaiah Miller, Rachel's father, stood before him.

"Daniel?" Isaiah almost sounded surprised to see him. Apparently, Rachel either hadn't been reading his letters or had neglected to tell anyone what was in them.

"Hi, Mr. Miller," Daniel began. "I know this is strange, but I'm out on good behavior. Is Rachel home?" At the mention of Rachel, Isaiah suddenly became vitriolic. His face became almost as red as the back of his sunburned neck.

"Listen here, you stay away from my daughter. She's finally happy and just got over you. She's found someone else, do you hear me? So stay out of her life!"

"Wait—" But it was too late. Isaiah had slammed the door in his face, leaving him on the doorstep with nothing but confusion. What did Isaiah mean that Rachel had *finally* moved on? Had she actually still been in love with him until recently? What changed her mind? Why didn't she ever write him back?

Before Daniel even had time to process what was happening, the door burst open again. He was expecting Isaiah Miller with a few more things on his mind, but instead got the object of his obsession for the past 2 years and the love of his life, Rachel.

"Daniel!" A smile quickly spread across her face as she flung her arms around his neck. After a moment, he finally returned the hug. Having just heard the news that she was taken by someone else, this was the least expected response, but he readily accepted it. Any form of physical touch from her was like refreshing rain on the desert of his soul.

Finally—with a little disappointment creeping in on Daniel's part—she pulled away and asked, "How are you? How did you get out?" She narrowed her eyes. "You didn't escape did you?" Daniel laughed, glad for some respite of happiness in the dreariness of his thoughts.

"No, I didn't escape. I was let out on good behavior, but I still have to see a parole officer." Rachel nodded absently, not quite comprehending what that meant since that wasn't something many Plain people had to deal with.

"Anyway, come in! Ignore Papa, he just doesn't want someone to steal me away from my new boyfriend." She cast a glance at someone on the other side of the door as she moved out of the way to let Daniel in.

"Yeah, he mentioned you had met someone else. Congratulations!" He said it with as much happiness as he could muster.

Rachel curtsied. "Thank you. Actually, it's kind of a funny story how we started going steady."

As Daniel moved into the house, he noticed that Mr. Miller was sitting in the old overstuffed chair on the other end of the living room (the object of Rachel's earlier sideways glance), and across from him on the couch was none other than Jeremiah's younger brother, Josiah Schwartz.

"Oh wow," Daniel finally mustered after another moment of shock. "Well, I guess we have to keep it in the family, eh?" He tried to make it sound like a joke, but it came across very much like an insult. Unlike his older brother, Josiah didn't even bother with the comment. Instantly he jumped up and gave Daniel a big hug as if they were the ones that had always been friends.

"Daniel King! Oh my goodness, it is so good to see you! And in good health!" He gave Daniel a slap on the back as Daniel returned the kind gesture. Out of the corner of his eye, Daniel saw Mr. Miller watching his every move like a hawk. Thankfully after over a year in penitentiary where someone was always watching, it wasn't so hard to get used to.

Daniel took Josiah's hand and shook it. "Yes, I'm in very good health. Congratulations to you on taking the finest woman in the entire world." Rachel blushed while Mr. Miller shifted in his seat protectively. Josiah only smiled wider.

"Thank you! Gosh it means so much to me that you approve. I know that you were originally promised to Rachel, and even though everything didn't go according to plan, I promise that I will protect her with my life... as you did with yours."

This gave Daniel some pause and he looked at Josiah questioningly. "You're not... mad about what I did?" Josiah laughed heartily as he sat back down and Daniel grabbed the wicker rocking chair that Rachel provided.

"Are you kidding me? That's a long time to be mad. Shoot, I can hardly be mad at the sun for doing its job now, can I?" Josiah leaned back and shook his head. "No, I'm not mad at you. But I am mad at Jeremiah. He knew what was right and what was wrong. We had just had an argument the night he left about what you had preached that Sunday morning out of Proverbs 20:1, 'Wine is a mocker, strong drink is raging: and whosoever is deceived thereby is not wise.' You had said in your sermon that it doesn't matter what anyone thinks, alcohol always wins the argument if you let it go into your body. We need to be on guard and abstain from the pleasures of the world like alcohol and tobacco, and instead focus on things that are pure and right."

Daniel was shocked that Josiah remembered so much detail from the sermon that morning and said as much.

"That argument was the last conversation I had with my brother," Josiah said matter-of-factly. The atmosphere in the room suddenly changed to something akin to gloomy before Josiah finished his thought. "Sometimes I wish I had just gone with him to talk him down. You tried to talk him down, didn't you, Daniel?"

The truth was, Daniel hadn't even attempted to talk at all. He had been so past the point of trying to reason with Jeremiah that he had determined the only way to get through to him was to knock him out. The only problem was that Daniel didn't know he had so much pent up anger from all of the previously fruitless encounters he had had with his best friend.

"He did everything he could to get Jeremiah to stop. He also just got a little carried away," Rachel answered quietly. The answer wasn't completely untrue, but in that moment, the last thing on his mind had been talking.

"I should go," Daniel said as he stood to leave. Turning to Mr. Miller he said, "Thank you for allowing me to come over." Turning to the couple he added, "I realize that my coming here was not only a waste of time but an interruption... which then turned into an interrogation. If you'll excuse me, I need to find somewhere to live."

At once, Rachel and Josiah raced to stop him from leaving.

"Alright!" For the first time since Daniel had stepped over the threshold of their home, Isaiah Miller spoke. "You're all acting like a bunch of children and this needs to stop. All of you, come in here and sit down!" Without hesitation, all three returned to their seats. "Now Daniel, I understand that you just got out of prison and the last thing you want is to be bombarded by questions, but we are all still feeling the effects of what happened. Josiah," At his name, Josiah jumped. "I know you've forgiven Daniel, but the rest of us are still struggling to come to terms with the fact that a killer is now walking among us." Isaiah put his hand up as Daniel started to protest. "And Rachel," At this point, Isaiah softened. "Sweetie, just be careful with your heart. You have two mostly good men to choose from, and I won't tell you what to do, but I will tell you this... I love you, and I'll support whatever decision you choose."

Isaiah pulled himself out of his chair and as he left the three, he stated, "Daniel, you can stay in the guest bedroom upstairs."

With some surprise in his voice, Daniel thanked him. How did Isaiah know he wanted to room with them?

As if in response, Mr. Miller called out from the kitchen, "Why else would you come to my house first?"

Rachel only giggled as Josiah and Daniel exchanged confused looks.

Within a few days it was obvious that the Miller's farm, which had once been the most productive farm in the community, was failing and needed help. As a tenant and old friend, Daniel had been drafted into helping in the field and in any way he could to keep the farm afloat. Even Josiah Schwartz had begun working for Mr. Miller for free as long as he had food to take home with him every night. These long days in the fields together made for a lot of discussions, debates, and discourses about God, life, and what everyone had been doing in Daniel's absence.

Daniel learned that his family had moved out of the community and no one had heard from them since, and that Rachel's mother had gone with them, taking Rachel's little brother Laban with her. In fact, that was the biggest reason the Miller farm was failing: many people began to suspect that Mrs. Miller had led something of a rebellion and took the King family with her. Other rumors included all of them committing mass suicide together, leaving the Plain life because it was too much, or simply leaving the community to try to raise money to get Daniel out of jail. The last one sounded the most likely since Daniel was now a free man, but he didn't give it too much thought. He just longed to see his mother again and sit by her side as she stroked his hair.

All wishing aside, being this close to Rachel for the first time in almost two years was the next best thing. Except it seemed that she had been avoiding him since that first day. When he asked her about it, she looked away and changed the subject. He finally decided to ask Josiah about it, so one day while they were out alone, he popped the question.

Josiah straightened and stretched from his task before answering. "Well," he began. "In short, she despises you. You killed one of her best friends, she didn't hear from you once while you were away, her mother and little brother ran off, and the farm is failing. She blames you for all of that."

"Wait a second, did you say she never heard from me?" Josiah nodded.

"That's what she told me."

"I wrote her every week just like I promised. I even wrote her the week I was released so she would know I was coming. She really didn't receive any letters?"

Josiah shook his head. "I'm sure of it."

Daniel spent the next few moments trying to figure out exactly what happened to his mail, only to be interrupted by a question from Josiah.

"Do you still love her?"

Daniel looked right into Josiah's eyes and said, "With all my heart."

"Then make the smart choice and stay out of her life for a while. I know you want to fix things, but she still has some issues she has to work through before she can really talk to you."

Daniel was confused. "How do you know that?"

"Because," Josiah said as he went back to his work. "The story of what happened that night has changed at least six times." He stopped working again to look at Daniel. "At first it was the small details that changed: where you were, where she was, who was around. Then it became bigger things: you tried to talk to Jeremiah before striking, Jeremiah wasn't drunk he was just confused and hurt…" He trailed off. Daniel wasn't sure because of the sunlight, but he thought he saw a tear run down his new friend's cheek. Daniel had had so many dreams of so many different viewpoints, but the story was always the same: Jeremiah was drunk, he charged them, Daniel struck first, struck hard, and pulverized his best friend's face.

"Are you alright?" Daniel turned to Josiah, who had asked the question, but realized his vision was cloudy.

"I will be one day. But today is not that day." Daniel returned to his work without another word.

Over the next few months, Daniel and Josiah had come up with a plan to turn the fate of the Miller farm around. By now the whole community knew that Daniel King was back and that Isaiah Miller had employed him. They were watching his every move, and he knew as much. Within the first week, he had made a public apology and had asked the preacher and local bishop for forgiveness. The bishop and the preacher granted it, but the rest of the community was still unsure.

However the new business plan Daniel helped implement really put him in a good way with the community as he began to turn everything around. The business plan included selling to the English towns surrounding the community, as well as holding what English people would call "farmer's markets" to draw them into the community to bring even some tourism revenue. In just a few short months, the Miller farm was once again one of the major points of the community, with Daniel King at the helm.

Daniel couldn't help but wonder about his absent family at this point. Would he ever be able to see them again? Where were they? Were they even still alive? Worrying didn't bring them back and he knew that, but he really wished he could see them... and that Rachel's missing family members would return as well. It didn't make sense for them all to run off for any reason, especially for Rachel's mother and little Laban. He would be 8 this year... if he was still alive that was. Daniel had begun to feel overwhelmed and although he wasn't much of a writer, he had been writing to his friend Bobby Meyers regularly and telling him about some of the things that had been happening good and bad. This day was different because Daniel finally got a letter back.

Hey Daniel,

I know this isn't much, especially after everything you've been writing to me lately, but the prison only allows so many letters to go out from one person at a time these days. I guess we had some anthrax scare... even though anthrax is so 2000. Anyway, glad to hear that the farm is doing better and that you're liking the lady's man well enough to be friends with him. It takes a real man to step aside and let someone else have a go... especially cuz I know how much you like her. Sounds like the best option might be for you to just let her go at this point. She doesn't want you that much and it would be a rough life for you staying with those people.

I mean, it's great and all that you're there and that you've been forgiven and redeemed yourself, but you gotta remember that Jesus is the the One Who really redeems. You don't need man's opinions to get through this life. Sometimes it sure seems like it, but really all they do is give you jobs you hate with people you don't like... so just be yourself and be willing to let Christ do His work in you.

OK, so I guess I got super sappy there for a second. Either way, I'm gonna close this letter since I'm mostly out of paper. Great job for squeezing the day!

Keep your eyes on the prize,

Bobby

Bobby had indeed written on a rather small piece of paper and taken up just about every inch of it. He might have commended Daniel for squeezing the day, but Daniel felt like he needed to commend Bobby for squeezing every bit of white off of this paper. He chuckled to himself trying to picture Bobby hunched over the table in his cell, writing as small as possible to fit as many words as the paper would allow. It was a humorous sight, since Bobby was even less of a writer than Daniel.

Daniel knew that Bobby had a point about staying there in the community, and although he really wanted to leave, he knew he couldn't—or wouldn't—be able to until he'd fully told his story. At this point, it was just a matter of when he would tell it.

The wedding of Josiah Schwartz and Rachel Miller was only a few days away and the community was busy helping in every and any way they could. There were people setting up decorations in the church, there was an entourage of people following both Josiah and Rachel around as they made their final preparations, and since neither of them had mothers to speak of, the women of the community came together to cook, bake, and clean the Miller's home. Daniel had learned a thing or two about baking during his time in prison; he was more than willing to help the women with the cake.

Right in the middle of putting the second layer on the cake, Rachel came into the kitchen. "Daniel, we need to talk." Daniel looked at Rachel briefly before bringing his focus back to the cake. One of the women, Lorelai Troyer, quickly came over and stole everything away from Daniel so that he had no option but to talk to Rachel.

"I'll be right back," he told the kitchen full of women.

As Rachel and Daniel walked out the back door and began walking around the yard, Rachel finally began to form her thoughts into words.

"Daniel, I just want to let you know something."

"OK, I'm listening."

Rachel paused for a moment. "I still love you."

Daniel stopped walking and looked Rachel in the eye, skeptical that he had actually heard correctly. "I'm sorry?"

Rachel sighed, "I know, it's silly." She turned and intended to keep walking, but Daniel grabbed her arm and spun her around. Without thinking about what he was doing, he was kissing her. It was a feeling he'd never experienced before since this was the first time he had ever kissed her. It was like every nerve in his body was at attention and he felt the hairs on the back of his neck stand up as if he was afraid. But he wasn't afraid, in fact, he felt more courageous now than he ever had. Rachel pulled away first, and slowly.

"It can't be like this," she whispered as their noses touched.

"I know," he responded in kind. He waited until he could force himself to pull away before telling her. "I'm leaving after your wedding. I'm going to gather the community together tonight and tell them the whole story... and then in a few days, I'll no longer be here."

Rachel looked deep into his eyes, searching for some sign that this was a joke. Finding none, she simply nodded as they turned and walked back to the house together. "Thank you for telling me," she finally conceded. "Does anyone else know?"

"You're the first... and the only one I wanted to tell." She looked at him with a fierce intensity.

"You have to tell the community you plan on leaving. They've come to trust you. Don't be like your family and my mother. Tell them what you plan on doing. At least hear out any suggestions they have." Daniel thought about it a moment, then smiled.

"OK. I'll do it for you."

With the help of the baking women, Rachel, Josiah, and Isaiah Miller, everyone in the community knew within an hour that Daniel King was to give a speech. Nobody knew what it was about, but love him or hate him, the entire community had grown to respect him. He had saved their community from having to send more of their children to get English jobs, and for that they would do almost anything for him. Daniel wasn't so sure how they would feel after he told them his story. As he walked up the steps of the church, he had a familiar feeling of guilt, shame, and fear come over him. He stopped just outside the church doors and breathed a quick prayer to the God of Bobby Meyers, if that God was even real.

If You're real, then send me a sign that You'll always be with me, he prayed haphazardly. Just then he heard movement behind him. He was sure everyone in the community was in the church... so who was behind him? Slowly he turned, and couldn't believe his eyes. His own mother, AnnaBelle King, stood before him in English clothes! And behind her was his little sister Annalise, his father David, and Rachel's mother and little brother! Suddenly his eyes filled with tears.

"Mom" was all he managed to get out before breaking down in full-fledged sobs as his mother pulled him into a hug and held him. They stood there for what felt like forever, and he was OK with that, because his mother was finally here for him. Nothing else mattered in that moment. She pulled him back to get a good look at him.

"Look at you, my darling son. So grown up. So mature. Your father and I always knew you would make the right choice in the end."

"What is the right choice?" Daniel asked as he pulled himself away and wiped his tears with his sleeve. Just then, Annalise came and gave him a hug, and the tears started to flow again.

By now, the entire congregation had heard the commotion outside and had gone to the windows to see what they could. From what Daniel could tell, there were cheers and applause going on inside, but he wasn't about to move from the door just yet for fear that the truly loved ones in his life would be vapors and would disappear as soon as someone else entered the picture. Without warning, the door burst open anyway and Rachel flew past him.

"MAMA!" As she fell into her mother's arms, with little Laban there, they held each other and wept. Annabelle smiled looking at them.

"Mary's been so worried about Rachel and Isaiah. I knew we were meant to come today."

"Mom," Daniel tried again. "You said you knew I would make the right choice, but I don't even know what that is."

David responded, "John 8:32, 'And ye shall know the truth, and the truth shall make you free.' By telling the community your story, you're releasing them from everything you've held against them, knowingly or unknowingly." Daniel looked at his mom and she nodded approvingly.

"How did you guys know this was going to happen? I only told Rachel just today."

"And Bobby Meyers in a letter," Annalise offered innocently. Daniel finally understood what had been happening.

"All of those letters that went missing, that was you." His mother nodded. "Why?"

His father answered, "Because we were looking for you, to figure out a way to get you out of prison. And then when you got out, we wanted to come for you, but as soon as we realized you had intentions of making things right, we decided it best to stay gone, at least until the right time."

"Why did you and Laban go?" Rachel asked her mother, who simply smiled.

"Because I always saw Daniel as one of my own children, and I thought he should still have the best life, even if it wasn't with you. You and your father are strong, I knew you could handle it. I'm only sorry I didn't leave a note telling you what happened." Rachel smiled as fresh tears welled in her eyes.

"It's in the past now, Mama. You're here, and you're well. That's all that matters. I forgive you."

Daniel finally came to his senses and remembered what he was doing. "I have to go in there."

As soon as he opened the door, the preacher was standing there with a twinkle in his eyes. "You don't have to tell us anything, young man. We've forgiven you, the whole community has. You've brought people together in a way few others could. You saved our community in its worst time and you even returned those that were lost to us. Whether you stay or whether you leave, you will always have a home here with us." There was a chorus of "amen's" and "here, here's" behind him.

Daniel didn't know what to say, so he said the only thing that came to his mind, "Thank you." In that moment, he remembered the prayer he had just prayed and realized that there was a God and He did care about Daniel King. "There is one thing I want to say in everyone's presence first. I forgive you, and release you from the hard feelings and bitterness that I've harbored against you for so long."

The preacher nodded. "As the preacher, I think I can speak for all of us when I say 'thank you.'" Again there was a chorus of agreements.

After a few moments, Mary sighed and said, "Now, let's finish with the preparations for the wedding! We only have a day left! Chop chop!"

And with that everyone went back to work as usual. But it wasn't usual anymore. Everything was different because the air was clear, and

Daniel felt a freshness in his bones that he had never felt before. He finally understood why Bobby was always so excited about life, because that's exactly how he felt. Even if he didn't get the girl, that wasn't the point of this venture. He did what he had been "commissioned" by his good friend to do: squeeze the day. There wasn't anything better he could ask for. For the first time in his life he was glad he didn't get the girl, because he would have been less happy and less open to Who God really was to him. It was an amazing and beautiful choice to finally live in the peace and contentment of God. And he loved every second of it. This was where he belonged, no matter what.

THE SHY AMISH BRIDE

NATALIE MEYER

Three best friends, Betty, Amity and Rachel are practically inseparable. But when they land themselves in a stormy predicament on their way home on night a newcomer in town comes to their rescue. All three girls show an interest in the handsome stranger, but only one of them would walk away with the prize. What starts off as nothing but a playful bet between friends, ends up surprising them all.

Uri Guth came to Derby Creek to start afresh, the last thing he expected was to fall in love. But when he meets the shy red head who reminded him autumn, he pulled out all stops. He knew the moment he laid eyes on her that she was his match.

Chapter 1

Rain just kept falling, never ending without any intention to stop, large puddles had gathered on the muddy grounds around the big barn, and water gushed down the eroded embankment running alongside the road, causing the road to be completely flooded. But no amount of rain would prevent Amity, Betty and Rachel to do what they came here to do. Having been friends since childhood, the three women were inseparable. Neither of them were married or promised to anyone yet, and although they are well beyond the age most girls in their community starts to settle down to start a family, it never really bothered them.

Amity was strong willed and mouthy young woman, who voiced her opinion whenever she felt it mattered. Of course her father, Bishop Gunther didn't quite approve of her behaviour at times, but he did support her willingness to stand up for herself. Bishop Gunther on the other hand wasn't like most others in their faith; he was more lenient and accepting than most, always promoting change within reason. He insisted that households started using gas stoves instead of coal stoves. He had even arranged to buy a truck to help the community to cart goods to the local market in town. According to him, modern change to a bare minimum does not give the devil a foothold, it just shows the devil that they are capable of change without modern ways ruling their lives and changing who they are or distracting them from things that matter most.

Betty, much like Amity also had a strong personality, one she definitely got from her mother, but she also had a mischievous streak. When the elders instructed the children not to play in the rain, she was always the first to splash in muddy puddles. When they had their social events, she was the one who would pull pranks, like stuff a mouse in someone's pocket or stick a dish to a table cloth with workman's glue, causing a huge disaster when someone tries to pick it up. All innocent pranks at most, but that was how everyone knew her and more often than not, when she was younger her father would ground her for punishment, but she always found a way out of it.

And then there was Rachel, shy quiet Rachel. More like the runt of the litter, she was one of few words and always just tagged along because Amity and Betty insisted. Rachel only had a father; her mother died giving birth to her. Her father eventually married Elsa, a widow with two sons, who she never got on with. They were two brats and she ended up spending more time with her friends than her own family and over the years, the trio had become the best of friends

Betty giggled and Amity squirmed on the bale of hay, "I bet you David looks like that when he takes his shirt off," she said pointing to the male model in the fashion magazine.

Amity giggled, "It's scandalous! If your dad knew you had these, he'll shun us all," she said in jest.

Rachel, curious as ever, was sitting on the left, also peeking at the magazine, one of the few they kept hidden in the barn under one of the wooden floor slats. They always snuck to the barn to page through the magazines and weigh every other man in their town up against the likes of models that posed so shamelessly with nothing but pair of underpants on.

"*Jah!* Well he doesn't know now does he?" Betty said and paged through a few more pages.

Rachel would never admit it out rightly but she also felt a slight tingle of excitement when she looked at these magazines, they were not overly crude, but they showed more flesh than she had ever seen in her life. Maybe it was because of this, that they were all still single, she thought. Comparing the local boys to those men were like comparing apples with onions.

A sudden noise quickly alerted them and Betty shoved the magazine behind the bale of hay they were seated on. Both Amity and Betty grabbed their egg baskets, while Rachel stood around looking as guilty as ever.

"Betty, are you girls here?"

It was Betty's father who called, and Rachel's stomach lurched, if the Bishop had any idea what they were up to they will be in so much trouble.

"We're here *daed*!" Betty called and dusted the hay off of her dress, "We were caught in the rain, and was waiting for it to pass," she said as her Bishop Gunther appeared.

"I thought so, well I have come to get you girls home, the storm is a long way from being over," he said and handed each of them a rain coat, "Better we hurry, or the storm will catch up with us," he urged them as he let each one of the girls walk towards the barn door ahead of him.

The sky was dark and it wasn't just a summer shower, it was a downpour that looked more like a waterfall from heaven. Heavy drops struck the ground tunnelling into the earth. Up ahead stood the buggy, which didn't offer much or any shelter and Rachel wasn't so sure if they would make it to their respective homes in one piece. Betty was the first to step into the rain, followed by Amity. Bishop Gunther looked at her and nodded, and then in a huddled group the four of them ran towards the buggy, careful not to slip and fall.

Thankful that there was still some daylight to guide the way, the three girls clung to each other as Betty's father steered the buggy towards the house. Hardly able to see a few feet ahead of them and on a treacherous road that has been washed away in most places, Bishop Gunther was still able to make them feel at ease. He didn't even look worried, but then again, that was probably how a man of God should be, like Paul walking on water.

The buggy wheels rattled as they rode over rocks and muddy trenches formed by the mass of water running diagonally across the small road. And a trip that normally took less than fifteen minutes to travel, now seemed like an eternity. They were slowly making their way ahead through the stormy downpour, unbeknownst to Bishop Gunther, the road up ahead had turned into complete sludge and the moment the buggy reached it, the wheels simply slid into a deep trench on the side of the road, pulling the buggy, with the horse off and on to the side of the road. The girls screamed in panic as the buggy slowly leaned over to its side, threatening to topple over. Rachel was the first to clobber out and then helped the other two on to the road. Betty got out safely, but as Amity stumbled out of the buggy, she stepped in a hole and twisted her ankle.

"Ow!!" she cried out as she fell to the ground grabbing for her ankle.

"Amity!" Betty cried and ducked down to help her friend, "Where does it hurt?"

Bishop Gunther also hunched down and looked at her ankle, "It's quite swollen, I think you may have sprained it, can you try and step on it?"

Betty and her father helped Amity to her feet, but the moment she put weight on her injury, she cried out in agony.

"We will have to get you home, just lean on me and Betty" the Bishop said. He studied the state of the buggy, "The buggy will have to stay here until morning."

"But papa, we can hardly see in front of us," Betty lamented as she supported her friend.

"The Lord will light our way," Rachel said confidently and gave Betty a gentle reassuring squeeze.

With Amity supported by Bishop Gunther and Betty, and Rachel next to them carrying the egg baskets, they started down the path taking carful steps in the dark.

Through the stormy gale and rain that kept showering, they heard a galloping sound that sounded more like thunder coming towards them and the next moment, a man on horseback arrived completely drenched.

Rachel couldn't make out his face, but right now he was the best thing that could have happened to them.

"Bishop, Maryanne sent me to see what was keeping you," he shouted over the raging storm, "What happened to the buggy?"

Rachel took over from the Bishop, while he explained to the stranger exactly what had happened, and suggested that they come to recover the buggy in the morning once the rain has passed.

"Betty, you will have to get on the horse with Amity, Rachel you will walk with Uri and I," the Bishop instructed and then the stranger named Uri, helped Amity, and then Betty on to the horse.

Together they slowly made their way back to society, the first stop was Amity's house, where the Bishop helped to get her inside, and seen to, then it was Rachel's turn and finally Uri, Bishop Gunther and Betty made their way to the Bishop's house.

~*~

After Rachel had changed into her night dress and towel dried her wet hair, she deposited herself in front of the fire place. The night had turned out a complete disaster. She was sure it was punishment for their bad behaviour. Lusting like that over fictitious men and so on. She wrapped her quilt around her shoulders and reached for her bible. She knew better than to let her judgement be influenced by anyone. Despite the guilt, she somehow found her mind drifting to the stranger who came to their aid. She still couldn't see his face clearly, but she was sure he was handsome, and strong.

She shook her head to chase away the thoughts and closed her eyes, and said a silent prayer of repentance. She was never going to look at those magazines again.

Chapter 2

The sun broke through the parted curtains in Rachel's room and she pinched her eyes shut. The night before had taken its toll on her, and resulted in her oversleeping when there was still so much to do. She was yet to feed the geese and get ready to go to the local market to deliver the eggs she had collected the day before, but she simply had no will power.

"Rachel!" Her step-mother called from the kitchen, "Come have your breakfast!"

Rachel covered her eyes with her forearm and sighed. She just needed a few more minutes of sleep, but she knew where her priorities lay. She willed herself out of bed and rushed around the room to get ready for the day. By the time she got to the kitchen her mother had already cleaned the dishes, and Rachel's breakfast was waiting.

"The Bishop and his friend were here earlier," Elsa commented in passing, "Looks like you girls had a rough night."

"Yeah, we got caught in the storm," she mumbled.

So the stranger is one of the Bishop's friends, which means he was old, she thought to herself.

"Apparently Amity had twisted her ankle quite badly, but she will be fine in a few days."

"I figured. She stepped in a hole when she tried to get out of the buggy, we couldn't see much."

Elsa came to sit at the table with her, "You girls need to be more careful, things could have been a lot worse."

Sometimes Rachel couldn't help but wonder what Elsa's agenda really was. At times she treated her like a stranger, barely paying attention to her, and other times she came across all motherly. And all this time Rachel had no choice but to keep her own emotions all bottled up.

"We will," Rachel said and stood up to wash her plate, "I'm taking the eggs to the market, is there anything you need me to do?"

"Oh not to worry about the eggs, I've already sold delivered them this morning."

Rachel felt as if she could crush the plate in her hands. Those eggs were her eggs, her income. She was saving money for herself, and now Elsa had taken the little bit she could earn for herself.

"Thank you," she said tight lipped without turning around.

"I hope you don't mind, your father does need some money to buy that new gas stove so, I figured every penny would help."

"Of course," Rachel turned around this time, with a fake smile plastered on her face, "I'll just get more eggs to get money for my new dress."

"Why on earth would you need a new dress?" Elsa said with mock surprise, "Don't you have enough as it is?"

Rachel was slowly starting to lose her temper, but she fought hard to remain calm, "I only have three dresses, and I need one for church, the others are all worn and faded."

Elsa laughed, "It's not like you'll be catching anyone's eye, and you're past the point of marriage. You're already considered a spinster."

"I'm only twenty-two, the same age my mother married," Rachel protested.

"And see how that turned out."

Elsa had barely said the words when her sons, Caleb and Alfred came into the kitchen, and Rachel had to hide her anger. She simply scooped up her empty egg baskets and stormed out of the house. How that woman dared say such heartless things and get away with it, was beyond her she thought as she marched determinedly in no particular direction. But as the anger subsided, it was replaced by doubt. Maybe it was too late for her to marry, but then the same applied to Betty and Amity, they were both the same age. Obviously living in Derby Creek wasn't much help either, there were far more women than men here, and unless they had gatherings from nearby towns, chances of finding a suitor was slim.

First of all there was Betty, who insisted that she was waiting for Mr Right, she refused to settle for less, then there's Amity who also had her own ideas of a suitor, and the few men that did ask for her hand in the past, were coldly turned down because she was just not interested. Rachel always thought that Amity was the kind who would go on a Rumspringa if her father allowed her, out of the three friends, she was the adventurous one.

Rachel grunted a loud oomph as she collided with someone sending her baskets flying. Thankfully they were empty; otherwise they would both have been covered in egg yolk. She stumbled back and started to apologize profusely when she swallowed her words, and a pair of very strong hands cupped her shoulders.

"Are you alight?" the young man asked, and offered her a lopsided smile.

"Jah, I am fine, I-I wasn't paying attention, I'm sorry," she said struggling to breathe.

"It's quite alright, you were miles away there for a second, I'm Uri, Rachel right?" he said and released her as he tucked his thumbs into his suspenders.

Uri, the name immediately rang a bell. He was Bishop Gunther's friend, but how? He was so young, she wondered.

"How do you know my name?" she asked foolishly.

"I came to your rescue last night in the storm, but I suppose you won't recognise me, it was rather dark."

"Oh! Oh right, yes. Well... um, I'll be going now. Thank you, I mean sorry, I... I have to go."

Rachel just about ran away from him, she had acted like a complete and utter fool, stuttering over her words like a second grader having to do an oral assignment. No wonder she was single. She couldn't sit in the company of a man without feeling awkward. As she hurried away she could feel his eyes burn into the back of her, but she refused to glance back. The farther she got away the quicker her out of control heart and raging butterflies would quieten down.

"Rachel!" It was Betty who waved her down, "Where are you heading?"

"Eggs!"

"You're going to Eggs?" Betty giggled.

"No, ugh, I'm going to collect eggs silly," she corrected herself as Betty fell into step next to her, "How is Amity doing?"

"She's fine, but you look like you've seen a ghost, why are you in such a hurry," Betty said as she tried to keep up to Rachel's pace.

"I need to sell enough eggs to buy a new dress. The cow sold all the eggs I collected yesterday."

"What a cow, did she not even ask you?"

"Does she ever?"

The rest of the way, the two friends walked in silence, Betty on her own planet, and Rachel trying to get Uri out of her mind. She hadn't expected him to be so young, nor did she expect him to know her name. The night before was a bit of a blur with everything going on, and she mostly remembered walking beside Bishop Gunther while Uri guided the horse by its reins with Amity and Betty on horseback.

"Is Uri your..."

"Don't you think Uri is..."

They both said at the same time and then burst out laughing.

"Uri is so handsome," Betty continued, "The last time I saw him was when we were kids. His family has been in Germany for the past few years."

"I didn't expect him to be so young," Rachel said, "Are they staying here?"

"Only Uri, he's staying at our house and is helping papa with a few things."

Rachel could hear by Betty's tone that she was keen on Uri, and she knew by the seam of her dress, that Amity will be just as taken by him.

One of them will most certainly catch his eyes, she thought and smiled softly. Her friends or at least one of them deserved a good strong man to care for them.

She dismissed the notion of Uri straight away, knowing that she would never stand a chance. She could hardly string together a proper sentence when she bumped into him earlier.

Chapter 3

Amity humped along with a crutch in one hand, while Betty excitedly skipped besides them. For the first time in who knows how long, Betty and Amity had made some effort to look presentable, both of them had brand new dresses. It was the Friday night frolic, where most boys got to voice their intentions.

Betty was nervous; as usual she was shy and nervous. She never liked these events much, she did not trust the thing called love, her father loved once, he had promised his her mother that he would make sure she was taken care of, but now years later, all she had to remember her mother by was a single letter, and a lifetime of regret. Elsa was kind in some ways, but she was jealous of Betty, and Betty never did much right in her eyes.

The people from the surrounding farms started to arrive, old and young, in the middle of the big barn the table was set as always. Food in excess was spread across the table, along with lanterns casting a dim glow over everything.

"Have you seen how handsome Uri is?" Betty whispered under her breath.

Amity giggled and shifted in her chair, "I know right? I can still feel his hands on my hips as he helped me on to the horse."

"Oh and weren't they the biggest stronger hands ever?" Betty swooned.

"I'm going to make a play for him you know?" Amity murmured under her breath.

"No you're not, I am, and I've already spent some quality time with him."

Betty wagged her brows and reached for bunch of grapes.

"You can't eat now, we have to say thanks first," Amity said slapping Betty's hand.

"Oh please, no one is even looking."

Betty listened to her friends as they cooed over the newcomer and she opted not to show any interest. They had reason to try and win his affection, she had none. She will see this night through and make the best of a bad situation. Besides, she had a lot more on her mind. Maybe it was time she accepted the fact that she was a spinster, and she figured it was time she spoke to the Bishop and go his take on her moving out of her paternal home into her own. She could always offer her help as a teacher. She knew how to read, in fact she loved reading. She could go spend time at the local school and read to the youngsters, even help the school teachers to give extra lessons in literacy.

"Rachel!" Amity's voice broke into her thoughts.

"Oh... sorry I wasn't listening," she apologised.

"I was saying, maybe all three of us should play for Uri, we can see which one he picks."

Rachel raised her brows, "He's not up for auction, it's a silly game you're wanting to play."

"Stop being such a drab! It will be fun."

No it won't, she thought. The first thing that is bound to happen is that Uri will pick either Betty or Amity, then that will leave one or the other angry and disappointed, ruining a friendship of many years.

"I'm not a drab, I'm just saying. What if he picks Betty, then you'll be angry, not?"

Amity rolled her eyes, "You take things way to seriously, if he picks Betty, then so be it, I'm hardly desperate to marry."

"Come on Rachel, it will be fun; besides, maybe he shows no interest in any of us, then at least we know we all tried."

Betty worried her lip and looked down at her hands, "I don't know, I suppose no harm can come of it." She for one knew that she won't be the least bit phased if he picked Amity or Betty, because she knew she stood no chance.

Amity shoved her elbow into Rachel's ribs and gestured with her head towards the door. Talk of the devil, Uri was heading straight down the path on the opposite side of the table with his eyes fixed on them. And once again the sight of him made her heart race and as she watched him approach it was as if all else around her faded. She had tunnel vision and it was only him looking straight at her. When he finally stopped and took a seat directly opposite her she averted her eyes immediately. Of course, Amity kicked her under the table and Rachel cleared her throat uncomfortably.

"*Hallo* Uri," she said.

"*Hoe gaan het*, Rachel?" he smiled.

She only nodded, her tongue felt like led in her mouth, and her palms were sweaty.

Betty and Amity both fell right into conversation, putting their best foot forward while Rachel wanted nothing but to flee. Soon enough the evening got on the way, with youngsters all frolicking and enjoying the event. Uri made sure he mingled with everyone and never let on that he was interested in any of them in particular, which was funny, since Betty put her best foot forward and out rightly told him he had beautiful eyes.

As the evening drew to a close and most of the people had left, the last remaining few spent the rest of the time talking about the up and coming barn raising event. Uri was still seated across from Rachel, and Betty and Amity had moved closer to where Bishop Gunther was. He was playing the harmonica, which was probably the only instrument allowed in the community, but still sounded like heaven.

"So Rachel, have you always lived here?" Uri asked curiously as he picked on some of the bread sticks on his plate.

"*Jah*, I was born here," she said and offered him a shy smile.

"I'm surprised I don't remember you?"

"I'm not exactly the most memorable of all," she laughed.

"Oh but you are, you are a very beautiful woman."

Rachel blushed profusely and covered the side of her face with her hand, "Thank you," she mumbled.

"Can I pick you up for church on Sunday?"

Shocked at his request, Rachel shifted uncomfortably in her seat and worried her lip, as tempting as it was, she wasn't so sure if it was a good idea. But then again, Betty and Amity did say that they should all try and win his affection. She looked down at her empty plate and smiled. Perhaps it was time she stepped out of her comfort zone and tried dating at least, after all, he was simply going to take her to church, and it wasn't like he was proposing to her at all.

"Sure," she said and then got up, "I have to go now. I will see you around."

She saw his mouth open and close, but she rushed away regardless. She said her goodbyes to her friends and the rest of the community who were all still in the barn and headed home. Her mind was racing and her heart even more. For the life of her she couldn't understand what Uri saw in her. *You're a beautiful woman* – he had said, and it made her feel as if she was about to fly into the night sky on wings of angels. No boy, or man for that matter, had ever paid her such a compliment, and coming from someone as handsome and Uri, made her tummy do strange things.

Chapter 4

Uri was up and ready long before dawn on Sunday, making sure his buggy was clean and that he too was dressed in his best church clothes. He couldn't deny the fact that he felt bad for Betty, she had shown her affection so openly, but there was just no chemistry between them. Unlike Rachel, Betty was just too flamboyant to his liking. She was a pretty woman, but not even nearly as pretty as Rachel. Rachel was unusually pretty, with red hair that always seemed so perfectly plated and rolled up under her prayer cap, with loose strands that tickled her cheeks. The slight dusting of freckles across her nose, that spread to her cheeks made her even prettier, almost innocent not to mention the way she blushed every time he spoke to her.

He was quite surprised when she accepted his request to start off with, but pleased nonetheless.

The first night he saw the shy girl, with her baskets filled with eggs, he was intrigued. She was in control despite the stormy weather and their predicament, and even when he lifted the other two on to the horse, she never uttered as single complaint. She walked quietly next to them as if she was taking a stroll. Not even the rain slanting heavily against them broke through her composure. Maybe it was the way she kept to herself, or the way her eyes lit up the next day when he bumped into her, he wasn't quite sure himself, but if he had to pin it to one thing, it was God's will. It was God's will that he returned to Derby Creek after all these years and God had sent the storm so that he could meet his future wife.

"Uri, you're up early," Betty said as she entered the kitchen where he was having his morning tea.

"Jah, up and ready for church," he said and grinned excitedly.

She came to sit next to him and perched her chin on her hand, looking at him all dreamy eyed. Shifting slightly to get some distance, he smiled and shoved the plate of rusks closer to her.

"I'm on my way to collect Rachel for church," he announced, not sure how Betty would react.

From day one, she had made it no secret that she fancied him; neither did Amity, so it was better if he got it out in the open before either of them got their hopes up.

"Rachel?" Betty said scrunching up her face, "Have you asked her then?"

He nodded and took the last sip of his tea, "Jah, she's a shy one, but she accepted my offer."

Betty scratched her head and slumped back in her chair, and Uri could just imagine what thoughts were flitting through her mind, hoping that this would not ruin their friendship. But when Betty stood up and held her hand up for a high-five, he grinned.

"She's a dear friend, but a nervous wreck, you best make sure you treat her right," Betty grinned, "She's had a lot of hardship with that stepmother of hers."

Uri frowned, tempted to ask about this stepmother, but held back. If anyone was going to tell him about Rachel, it was Rachel herself. He would want for no secrets or tall tales to come from anyone other than her.

He looked at the clock against the wall in the kitchen and took his hat, nodded at Betty and headed out. For a man nearing his thirties, he felt like teenager himself.

~*~

Rachel waited outside for Uri's arrival and her stomach was doing wild flips, while her heart was missing beats every so often trying to keep up the pace. She had never entertained the advances of a man, and had no idea how to behave in the presence of one who had made his intensions clear. A boy simply did not offer a girl a ride in his buggy unless he was interested in her as more than a friend. This was serious business. She also omitted to let her father know, because she knew that Elsa would have a hundred and one things to say about it. She shifted on the swing chair changing her position, trying to find the one that made her feel most at ease, but her body felt awkward. Her arms felt as if they were too long, her legs felt numb and overall her body and mind appeared to be disconnected. Tired of trying to figure out the best seating position she stood up and paced up and down the porch, and then finally she opted for leaning against the pillar. Just in time too, as she heard the nearing rumble of a buggy, which could only have been Uri.

When he came to a stop in front of her gate, she quickly rushed down the stairs.

"Morning Rachel, you look lovely today," Uri said as he climbed out and came around to help her in.

"Good morning," she said softly.

"Did you sleep well?"

"Jah, I did, thank you."

It took her some time to loosen up and say more than four words at a time, but Uri had this amazing ability to make her feel free. With him she didn't have to count every word, or watch her tongue. She could just say what she wanted. On their way to church, he asked her about the things she likes most. The talked about her life, and her family, she didn't feel like she needed to hide anything from him at all. She even admitted how she felt about Elsa, which made her feel less restricted. At church, they didn't sit next to each other, but Betty and Amity were curious as ever.

"So he picked you did he?" Amity whispered under her breath.

"I don't know, maybe," Rachel murmured.

"You're blind as a bat; everyone can see he likes you."

Rachel blushed and kept her head down, her friends were impossible and as much as she tried to pay attention to the service she couldn't. If it wasn't for Betty or Amity, whispering to her under their breaths, it was the sure awareness of Uri watching her. And that did not go unnoticed by her friends either.

By the time the service had come to an end, Rachel couldn't wait to get outside to catch a breath of fresh air, and steal a moment for herself, but it was short lived.

"You never told us you're meeting a boy?" Elsa said as she came to stand next to Rachel.

"I didn't know I needed your permission," Rachel said blankly.

"Well I suppose you are old enough to make your own, but you know, Albert will be very disappointed that you never told him."

Rachel knew exactly what Elsa was playing at, and this time she was not going to let the woman who pretends to care throw any hurdles in her way.

"I think he'll live, and you should be too pleased that I won't be a bother to you for much longer."

Talk about rushing into things, Rachel thought as she hurried away from Elsa, it wasn't as if Uri was going to ask for her hand in marriage, they hardly knew each other. But even if that wasn't the case, whatever happened, come the beginning of winter, she would move out anyway and start her own life, with or without a husband.

Chapter 5

Uri had spent most of the time getting to know Rachel, and the more he got to know her, the more he was convinced that she was the perfect wife for him. He had spent almost every evening visiting with Rachel and in the past few months since they started their courtship he got to know a woman, who despite her adversities in life, rose above it all. Her stepmother no longer tried to boss her around, and her father was too pleased that his only daughter is finally blooming.

It was a perfect autumn day; the ground was covered in a carpet of reds and golds that reminded him of Rachel. He had already asked her father for her hand in marriage, and although it didn't quite follow the custom of dating for an extended period, he saw no reason to wait. They were both adults who were in love and certain of one thing, their own happiness.

As usual he waited patiently for Rachel to exit the house, and like two curious toddlers Amity and Betty was not far away either. They had both come to terms with the fact that he had made his choice, and they were extra supportive of Rachel too. As he whispered a silent prayer for guidance, Rachel made her appearance as if the Lord had answered his prayer. Today was the day he was going to ask her for her hand in person.

"Good morning Uri," she said and her smile lit up his world.

"Morning to you Rachel, you look absolutely radiant today," he complemented her and it earned him an even wider smile.

"I made myself a new dress, do you like it?"

"It's beautiful," he said and held out his hand.

He could already imagine the gasps and giggles coming from the two friends as he struggled to find the right words. He had rehearsed it so well, but now here in the moment, he was at a loss for words.

"Are you alright?" she asked and placed the back of her hand against his cheek, "You look flustered."

Uri cleared his throat and caught her hand, keeping it against his cheek, "I'm fine, but there is something I would like to ask you."

Rachel tilted her head and her hazel eyes sparkled with curiosity as she waited for him to speak.

"Go on!" Betty shouted from across the road!

Uri closed his eyes and smiled, they weren't helping him at all.

"Uri?" Rachel said softly, "What is it?"

He took a deep breath, and then took both her hands in his, "Rachel, I have spoken to your father, and I would be honoured if you would agree to become my wife."

The way Rachel's expression changed from being concerned to completely surprise was priceless. She didn't have to answer him at all, because the way her lips tugged into a wide smile and her eyes filled with tears, he knew she wouldn't turn him down.

Rachel flung her arms around his neck and buried her face in the crook of his neck and whispered, "I thought you'd never ask."

Uri chuckled, "I was hoping you would accept."

"Why would I not?" she said and smiled lovingly up at him.

JOANNA

TORI BUCKLEMEYER

61

1.

Tracing her finger over the cold, gray tombstone, Joanna inhaled deeply and choked back a sob. Kneeling in the pasture of their family's cemetery, she placed a bouquet of daffodils in front of the stone. It all felt like a dream to her. She didn't think she would ever lose her mother. She was her best friend and now that she was gone Joanna felt lost. She spoke softly to the stone just as she would as if her mother were standing beside her. "Hello, Mother. I miss you more each day. I really wish you could have stayed. It's lonely here without you. Everyone is trying to be strong. They want to continue life as it was before, but without you being here, it's impossible. I know you're in a better place and you're not in pain from the illness ravaging your earthly body, but it's still hard. I just don't know what to do now. I have assumed all of your household duties, just as you would have wished, but I find myself feeling increasingly empty. None of this feels right." Before she could finish her conversation, she heard the distinctive sound of horses clopping in the distance. She knew her brothers would be coming to take her back to their small home in the center of their community. They would have finished their errands in town, and she would be needed soon to start preparing supper. Dusk would be upon them soon, and after evening services, a good meal, a nice fire, and sleep would be arriving soon.

Joanna stood up slowly and ran her fingers along the cold stone one more time, giving a weak smile of recognition to her brother, Eli, who trotted up on his prized horse, Petunia. Petunia was a gentle creature and was easily broken. Eli was good to the creature and she respected him as well, she wouldn't ever buck him off, even when they were traveling through thunderstorms or if she ran up on a snake in the tall weeds. They trusted one another. Joanna could say the same about her brother, even though she was the older sibling, they trusted one another and vowed to always protect one another through all of life's trials. Eli looked down from Petunia and frowned. He hated to see his sister suffer so, but as a young man, he knew that for the good of the community he couldn't let his own sorrows show. He had to be strong for his sister now and show nothing but unconditional support. Now was the time for them to come together as a family and keep each other close. That's what his mother would have wanted. "It's good to see you, sister. Are you ready to return to the house?"

Joanna looked up at Eli's eyes and knew that behind the deep brown spheres, there was a touch of sadness that lingered there. He was trying so hard to put on a brave front, but she knew the truth, he wouldn't be the same after their mother's passing either. "Yes. I'm ready to return, Eli. Can I ride with you?"

"Of course. I think Petunia has it in her to walk us both back home along the path." The horse merely whinnied and they both laughed at her response. As they trotted along the path, Joanna's voice turned solemn once again as she asked, "How's father today?"

"He didn't say much at all, he merely got up and went into his study, where he read some scriptures and made some notes for service, then he walked out into the garden and surveyed the crops. It was like a typical day for him it seems."

"I wish he would express himself more."

"Ah, you know how he is Joanna, that's how he always was, stoic and stone-faced."

"Yeah. Maybe one day we'll figure him out."

"Ha! You have jokes, my sister. I seriously have my doubts about that."

They rode back up to the house in relative silence only listening to the sounds of the birds chirping and the echo of Petunia's hooves against the ground. Reaching the house, the pair dismounted and Eli walked Petunia to the barn, taking care to make sure she had plenty of fresh hay and water. Joanna went straight into the house and immediately made her way to the kitchen. In her mind's eye, she could still see her mother standing by the stove, stirring a pot or leaning over to get a knife from the bottom drawer. It was up to her now to make sure the family was fed. She sighed heavily and reached up above the family's ice box to take down a larger pot which hung above it. It was cast iron and the same one that had been used in the family for generations to make hearty stews and soups. That night Joanna decided she would make the family a hearty beef stew. They had some extra meat frozen already in the icebox and she had plenty of canned vegetables from the summer and fall's gardening. She poured some water that had already been carried inside into the large cast iron pot and lit the fire beneath their wood and coal stove. When it came to a full boil she added the meat and vegetables. Her mother had always tried to make her stews last for a few days and made it a point to ensure it was filling as well. Joanna added some corn starch to thicken the broth and proceeded to flavor it with spices. When her father walked into the kitchen, he hung his head, but then looked up and met Joanna's eyes, giving her a slight nod of approval. When the preparations were finished Joanna carried the pot along with some freshly baked bread out to the dining room. The family took their assigned places around the square table. In their mourning period, it was customary to set an extra place at the table for the lost as well, so her mother's chair while empty next to her father, had a place setting and was served some stew as well. It would be her father's task to consume it.

2.

After all was seated, her father spoke. "Good evening my son and daughter. Let us all rejoice and give thanks for what the day hath brought forth. Now is the time we must graciously give thanks for the abundance the Lord hath provided us with and draw close together as a family in our hour of need. I was reading the scriptures this morning and they brought me much comfort. Despite our loss, I trust each of my children to go on living and continue to be upstanding and show true grace. Now let us break bread and honor the fallen."

They all opened their eyes and lifted their heads watching their father who broke the first bit of bread. He then passed the plate to the others who took their portions and set the tray back in the center of the table. Their meal was eaten in silence and no one dared to speak until their simple supper was finished. Their father then looked at each of them and smiled. Tufts of white hair showed his age and he had a natural ruddiness to his skin tone that made him look jovial. He also had lines etched along his forehead left by the many years of being contemplative. One would look at him and assume he was a stern man all of the time, but he had crows feet and smile lines along his eyelids that told another story. While their father was stern and quiet, Joanna could remember a time when they were children he would play their games with them and tell stories which made all of them laugh joyously. He was a man dedicated to worship, but he also was a man who prided himself on the family he had created.

Rising from the table Joanna began to gather the dishes and place them in the kitchen sink, as she crossed into the other room she heard her father say, "Joanna, I'm very pleased with all the progress you have made in the kitchen with meal preparations. Your mother, rest her soul, would be very proud of you." Tears formed in Joanna's eyes and she bit her bottom lip to choke back a sob. Her mother, Annabelle, had been gone now for over a month, but the loss still stung. Her entire family was stuck living with the reminders of her being. Joanna still hadn't had the heart to clean out her closet or her sewing room. The elders had planned a town gathering at the end of the month, however, so she thought she would take them then and donate them. After all, she was a practical woman, just like her mother before her, and knew that there was no sense in good pieces of clothing going to waste when someone less fortunate could be using them. She responded to her father when returning to the table for a second trip for the remainder of the dishes. "Thank you father, I appreciate it. I discover more techniques every day. I feel personal growth is important, don't you?"

"Why, of course it is, Joanna. I've watched you and Eli grow through the years and I'm proud of both of you. I personally feel comforted by the fact that no matter how many times I go to complete a task and fail, I always have another opportunity to give it another try. That's the beauty in salvation and forgiveness. As humans, we all fall short of perfection, but there's always the chance to redeem yourself through prayer and multiple attempts."

Eli cleared his throat and spoke for the first time since they arrived home. "I'm glad for that. I know that there have been many times I felt lost or like I was on the wrong path, but I would pray about it and then something would happen or suddenly change in my life." Joanna listened to the pair talk from the kitchen while washing up the supper dishes and smiled. She loved her father and brother dearly but felt lost. She had no one to talk about her daily affairs with now that her mother had passed. She couldn't tell her father about the gossip she overheard while getting notions for sewing. She couldn't talk to her brother about a certain feeling she had in the pit of her stomach when she watched the baker's son splitting wood while hanging their linens out to dry.

She listened as their conversation continued. Her father spoke in a good-natured tone and there was nothing condescending in his voice as he elaborated on the subject matter with his son. "Eli, do you remember that time you came home crying when you were thirteen or fourteen? It was late in the evening and mid-summer. You had just returned from Mrs. Hollister's barn dance, she was having to raise money for the local town orphanage. You came to me and had tears in your eyes and your lips were swollen and shaking. I'll never forget how dejected you looked."

"Yes, father. I remember that well. I had gone to the dance and got quite upset when I saw Pamela Davison dancing with my friend, James."

"Do you remember what I told you?"

"No, I can't say I can recall, though it must have worked, I haven't harbored feelings for Pamela since that night."

"What I told you then son, was that sometimes we think we know what's best for ourselves, but in the end, it's not us who is ultimately in control of that. Our actions may influence our day to day activities, but it is only through faith we can fulfill our ultimate destiny. Our almighty father wants us to be happy, but sometimes we have to learn a lesson the hard way so we don't pursue other things. Your courtship with Pamela, for example, is one of those things. Do you know what she's doing now?"

"No, father. I haven't a clue."

"She decided to go live among the outsiders. Her life has not been beneficial from it, given my understanding. The last news we received in a letter that she decided to pursue her career as a professional dancer. It turns out that career path led her to work in a nightclub for exotic dancing and she's developed a drug addiction. It's in my best estimation that she will more than likely spend a great deal of her life in prison for drug related crimes or prostitution. So, son, as you can see sometimes our Father doesn't answer our prayers for a reason."

"What if I could have changed her? If she stayed with me, then maybe she would have just lived her life pursuing the path of righteousness."

"Well, I know how susceptible young men are to the wiles of women and their charms. I think that given the choice, you would have left and gone with her and been corrupted by the outside world as well. Outside of our community, there is a temptation to pursue wrongdoing on every corner. No matter what your vice, there is some way to purchase it or attain it there. Never forget that on your travels, Eli."

"I won't Father."

3.

Joanna listened to their conversation while she continued to tidy up the dinner dishes. She knew that her mother would have loved that their father was attempting to socialize with his children, but she also knew that her mother would have played devil advocate in the conversation. She wasn't like most of the other women in the town. She was outspoken and often had heated debates on matters of faith or business with her father, yet they worked to balance each other out very well. Joanna was convinced that when God made her mother, his creation was done purely to spite her father and keep him in line.

She cleaned up the sink and then decided she would go ahead and get the percolator ready for the morning's coffee. She knew that would be the first thing their father would ask for when he woke up in the morning. He often preferred the strong brew first thing, then would go out to complete his chores, foregoing breakfast until their animals had been fed. He always said that if one took care of the animals, they would, in turn, take care of you. He lived by this strict routine day in and day out, with little variation in routine, save for the day he celebrated his wedding anniversary with his wife. On that day, both their father and mother would take a rare trip to town, where they would return with not only small gifts for the children but some goods, that were less costly to purchase such as new blades for the farming equipment. Joanna always dreamed of the outside world as being some type of magical realm where everyone had access to things like running water and life was easy, but as she grew older she realized the outsiders weren't much different than those in her own community. She wasn't allowed to do much traveling into town, but when she did she just noticed that the outsiders seemed to base their own value on their material belongings. This concept just simply didn't exist in her community, everything was shared.

Joanna saw that it was dark now outside and with her chores attended to, she didn't see the point in staying with the menfolk talking around the dinner table. Drying her hands on a dish towel, she decided to go ahead and excuse herself. Walking around the side of the table she approached her father and placed her hand on the side of his chair then leaned over kissing him on the forehead. "I'm going to go ahead and turn in for the evening, father. The nightly chores are all completed."

"Ah, yes, very good little one. My precious daughter. You have sweet dreams and remember that your father and brother are here if you have night terrors."

"Oh, papa. I love you. I haven't had a night terror, though, since I was seven years old."

"Still.. think good thoughts."

"I will. Goodnight. Goodnight Eli."

"Goodnight, sister, remember I love you even in your slumber."

"I will."

Joanna walked to her bedroom and lit the small candle that was on her nightstand, it provided enough light to read by, which is the only thing she enjoyed doing in the evenings to relax. Taking off her bonnet, she sat on the edge of the bed and began undoing the long braids she had in her hair. She preferred to keep it pulled up and away from her face during the course of the day since she was often doing chores. The tresses undid themselves easily and she fluffed hands through it, taking her hairbrush and running it through her long brown locks. After she put on her nightgown and hung her daytime dress back up in her standing closet, she picked up her Bible, seeing the notes she had made in the margins. She had been studying a chapter in Revelations that her father recommended. He felt that it would benefit the family to examine the reasons for death together, so they could make some sense of their mother's unexpected passing. She sighed and remembering her place decided she would finish reading and analyzing the chapter when she arose the following morning. Instead, she picked up the paperback she had borrowed from the town's library. It had a handsome cowboy on the front of it and he appeared in front of a herd of galloping horses. He was holding a blonde woman in his arms and she was swooning. Joanna smiled as the opened the book to the place she left off. It wasn't customary for women in her community to read much at all, but she enjoyed the thoughts of romance and found nothing wrong with dreaming about a handsome cowboy of her own. She finished the chapter and blew out her candle, reclining on her twin bed and closing her eyes sleeping almost immediately.

4.

As the dawn peeked through the clouds, Joanna was awakened by Eli, barging into her bedroom unannounced. He let the door bang on the hinges and had a panicked look on his face, as Joanna pulled the covers up over herself asked, "Why, Eli?! Whatever is the matter?! Is it Father?! Is he okay?!"

"Yes. Oh, Joanna, I'm worried. It's Petunia. She's fallen ill I'm afraid. Can you come out to the barn?"

Breathing out a sigh of relief, Joanna nodded and said, "Of course dear brother. Don't be fearful. The Lord will protect Petunia. Give me a few moments to get decent and I will be out there." Joanna calmly got up from her bed and walked to her closet, taking a few moments to pull her hair back and put on her bonnet then putting on her daytime dress. She pulled the laces tight on her boots and hurried out to the barn where she could see Eli standing by Petunia's stall pacing anxiously. "Thank you for coming out sister. I can't figure out what's wrong with her. She won't respond to my coaxing and she's just lethargic. I've never seen her in this state."

"Calm yourself, Eli. Your panicked state is doing her no good either. Animals can sense your fear." Joanna walked up to the mare who was laying down and looked into Petunia's deep brown eyes. She then placed her hand gently on the creature's forehead. She then stroked the animal's head and back, making soothing sounds, just as her mother would do them when they were sick youngsters. "Yes. You're right to have come to fetch me. She's definitely fallen ill. Let's just hope its a bug. Father has a trip planned to go into town to gather some new ax blades for the fall cutting. I'll go with him and stop by the library and see if I can find a cure in some of the veterinary medicine books they have shelved. Don't worry, brother. We will do what we can for her. Just be fervent in your prayers and there will be a way delivered."

Joanna walked back into the home and began preparing her father's morning coffee. Daylight had just broke and she knew he would be happy to get the day started like normal. When he walked in the kitchen he smiled seeing her standing at the stove as her mother would have, fixing his coffee and preparing breakfast for her brother. Eli always had a voracious appetite She set the steaming mug in front of him and said, "Good morning, Father. I must confess it's already been eventful."

"Oh, really how so?"

"It seems Petunia has fallen ill. I was hoping it would be okay if I went with you while you were in town today to look up some medicine for her at the library."

"I certainly hate to hear that Petunia has taken a turn for the worse. She has been good to our little family. I think that's a wonderful idea darling. God can work miracle cures, but only if we're willing to do a bit of the work as well. After the morning feeding, we will go into town. Be prepared. While I'm purchasing the new blades for the fall wood harvest, you can look into a cure for our Petunia. I bet your brother is worried sick."

"Oh, he is Father. You know he's always been close to the mare."

"We shall do what we can. Thank you for the finely brewed cup of coffee. Now I must get to work, the daylight is already streaming upon us and the chickens will be happy to receive their breakfast."

"Thank you, Father."

Joanna finished making the biscuits and gravy for breakfast then poured them all glasses of freshly squeezed orange juice from the assortment of oranges that they had traded for in town earlier in the summer. She knew their shelf life would be expiring soon and didn't want anything to go to waste. Waste not, want not, her mother always said. She also knew that they all need to keep their strength up because as soon as they got back from town the entire community would gather and chop wood for their collective heat in the winter. After completing her chores and cleaning up the cooking utensils she set the meal on the dining room table and gathered her bag for their trip into town. She made certain she had her city library card and decided to take her paperback with her and exchange it for another as it was nearing completion anyway. Looking around the empty room she sighed. She was worried about her brother, but also she felt a doubt creeping into her soul and a generalized discomfort, wondering if this is how the remainder of her days would be spent, taking care of her father and brother , never knowing the love of a man or having her own family to raise.

Her father and brother came back into the house after feeding the animals and sat down at the table, nodding in appreciation at having their meal already set before them. Eli spoke then, asking to say the morning prayers and included a blessing for his favorite mare as well. They ate the rest of their meal in silence and Joanna immediately went to the sink and began cleaning up the dishes, so she wouldn't have to do both the breakfast and dinner dishes before bed. She also was anticipating having a busy day tending to Petunia upon their return. Her father came and got her when the horses were hitched up to the wagon and her brother helped her climb in beside him. Her father gave his horses a quick pat on the head and they departed on their journey into town.

5.

Arriving in the nearest town, Joanna took in her surroundings as her father hitched up the wagon to the hitching post by the hardware store. She got out of the buggy, amidst the stares of the townspeople. She imagined she looked quite strange to then in her pale blue day dress, with her hair pinned up in a bonnet, while her father was dressed head to toe in all black, complete with his wide-rimmed black hat. His long brown beard wasn't shaved, merely groomed and it did betray his age, as spots of gray could be seen in it when the sun hit it just right. He spoke briefly to his daughter before going inside the store. "Remember daughter, be polite to the townspeople, but do not engage in lengthy conversation unless it pertains to spreading the Gospel. I will be here when you are ready to leave but try to find the information you seek quickly. I suspect this lost time will hurt our productivity later and we won't be able to get as much done as we should. Be careful, Joanna."

Joanna nodded and hugged her father before crossing the street and rounding the block heading to the library. She cast her eyes downward mostly only looking up periodically to dodge obstacles. She opened the doors to the city library and the pleasant librarian smiled and waved at her when she entered. She smiled back and returned the greeting. She liked the librarian, who never questioned her when she came in even as a little girl clutching her mother's skirts. The older clerk would give her lollipops when her mother checked out her religious books and romance novels. Now Joanna was grown and even though she didn't get a lollipop, she still felt those warm feelings when she was in the library. She walked up to the desk and quietly dropped her book on the counter. "I need to return this, and I will be getting another one if I can find the other information I need in time."

"Sure thing, Joanna. Have you been doing okay, since your mother's passing?"

"Oh, yes we have been doing alright, thank you. I'm sorry I was in such a bad state when you saw me last. I am adjusting to this new normal."

"Well, that's good. If you need anything, you let me know as always."

"I will. I will see you when I return."

Joanna then walked off, smiling once more at the clerk. She rounded the corner to the reference desk where there was no clerk, but there was a younger looking man in grease-stained coveralls standing by the finance books, looking bewildered. Joanna watched him pull out a book from the shelf as the rest came tumbling down. She couldn't stifle a small giggle as he fumbled trying to catch them all. He turned around hearing her laughter and she was met with a sheepish smile and the most striking blue eyes she'd ever seen. He took her by surprise as she felt her heart beat faster within her chest and suddenly heat rose to her face as she blushed deeply. Before she could say a word he smiled broadly at her and said, "They don't make these shelves the way they used to do they?"

Joanna giggled once again and said, "No. They certainly don't."

"I don't really know much about this place. I needed a book on taxes, I own my own mechanic shop and I'm doing my own this year to save money for the business. Maybe I should have just paid someone."

"Well, what are you looking for? Maybe I can help."

"A book to tell me how to do it."

Joanna paused for a moment surveying the shelves then reached down to the bottom one, accidently brushing the man's hand as she picked up a hefty volume and placed it in his arms. "Here you go. This will guide you through the process."

"Oh wow. Thank you. I appreciate that ma'am. It's nice to meet you, my name's David."

"I'm Joanna. I'm not from around here, as you can tell."

David took a step toward her, closing the distance, and Joanna felt a certain electricity pass through them. She let the heat rise to her cheeks again and once more looked into his blue eyes. He was in good shape and looked strong from his work. He had blonde hair and was clean shaven. He didn't look like any of the men from their community, but he did seem to possess the same kindness behind his eyes and good spirit. He responded by saying, "I wish you were from around here. I'd hire you to do my taxes."

She chuckled at his joke, then suddenly remembered her purpose. "I really hate to cut on conversation short, David, but I have to get some information then return to my community, my brother's horse is sick and needs medical attention I know nothing of."

"Oh, I'm sorry to hear that. Maybe I can help. I grew up on a ranch."

She couldn't believe her ears. She had wanted a cowboy all of her own. Could it be that her prayers had been answered? He seemed so genuine and caring. She explained the problem with Petunia and David gave her the information she needed to attend to the mare. He reassured her it was nothing major that some tender loving care couldn't fix. He then went on to say that his specialty in life was fixing broken things. Joanna considered the gravity of his statement before turning to leave and decided to do something she would need to ask forgiveness for later.

"You have been so helpful David, could I have your address?"

"Only if I can have yours too."

The pair exchanged addresses and Joanna exited the library, turning around to see David staring at her making her exit. She didn't know what had come over her, but she knew in her heart this man was her destiny.

6.

She exited the library to find her father standing red-faced by the door, checking his pocket watch. She hadn't realized how much time had passed talking with David, she only knew that it felt like they had known each other a lifetime. Feeling the need to apologize she spoke to her father, when they crossed to the buggy, "I'm sorry, father. It took me longer to get the information I needed than what I thought."

He didn't say anything, but merely nodded and coaxed the horses out of the lot and towards the path back to their community. Her father finally spoke when they were close to the halfway point between town and their village. "You know why we caution each other when talking with townspeople? It's not because our religion has restrictions on being social and making friends. In fact, we are encouraged to witness to everyone we possibly can. It's because not all people are righteous, Joanna. Not everyone will have your best interest at heart, and the original evil does find its way into the hearts of men. Some of the people you encounter in the outside world, well let's say the majority of them, only are interested in preying on the weak. It's their life's goal, not helping others or doing good."

Joanna turned her eyes downward again as her father patted her on the leg continuing, "Remember, no matter what happens, Joanna, your family will always support you within the community. We, however, could not help you should you decide to live among the outsiders. You would be shunned and on your own, you know it's our way, there's no changing that." Joanna nodded in acknowledgment, silently rubbing the piece of paper in her pocket which had David's address on it. She knew in her heart, that she needed to see the mysterious cowboy mechanic once again, but didn't like the idea of her father's disapproval. He would never allow such a thing, she felt conflicted and sick at heart the entire way home.

Arriving back at the community they were greeted by Eli, whose worried look had only grown more exasperated during their time away. "Greetings, Father. Greetings, Sister. Did you acquire the knowledge you sought?"

"I did brother. Let's go to the barn and see what we can do."

Together they walked to the barn and checked on Petunia. Joanna took care to follow David's precise instructions and administered a careful mixture of salt brine and water to the mare who greedily lapped it up. It had seemed that she had just gotten a bit dehydrated during their previous days' activities and was feeling under the weather. They monitored her condition throughout the day and it did improve as she eventually got up and started wandering back and forth in her stall, anxious for a trot. In addition to that the new blade purchase, expedited the wood cutting process and the community made short work of the wood pile, stockpiling enough wood to last the entire winter in half the time it normally would. They decided as a community to celebrate their recent accomplishment and give thanks to the Lord, with a feast to be held that upcoming Saturday night.

Joanna spent the night quietly in her room after supper and allowed herself to think of David. She knew beyond a shadow of a doubt that she needed him in her life. She believed, despite her father's warnings that there were good and decency in his soul. No one without a good heart, would have freely given her that information she needed to help her animal. Most of the outsiders would have offered their services and charged a pretty penny for such knowledge. Joanna thought of the feast Saturday and sighed. Did she want to be stuck in the community all her life, eventually marrying a man who had little passion for anything in life? It was then Joanna made her decision. She would slip away during the barn dance on Saturday and go see David.

As the community was abuzz with the festivities at the dance on Saturday night, Joanna excused herself to go back to the house, hugging her brother and her father tightly before exiting, saying she felt ill and needed to call it an early night. Unnoticed by anyone else in the community, she then proceeded down the well-worn path and made her way to town. She made her way to the address David had scrawled on a ripped piece of an envelope from his coveralls and knocked on his door.

David opened the door, rubbing his eyes, apparently awakened by her rapping. He was groggy but smiled broadly in recognition. "Joanna, is that you are am I dreaming?"

"No. You're not dreaming, David. I'm really here." She paused a moment, considering her options. She thought for a moment about what advice her mother would give her in this moment. She thought back to when she was a little girl clutching on to her mother's skirt, frightened by some imaginary threat. She would have said, "Ah, my precious little girl, there is nothing to be afraid of but your own imagination. If you don't give your fear power over you, you can achieve anything you want in this lifetime." Joanna hesitated a moment then said to David all while blushing and smiling, "I came to be with you David, and hopefully one day be your wife."

David took Joanna by the hand and led her over his front stoop, making sure she didn't trip over the door sill on the way in. When he shut the door behind her he pulled her into his arms and kissed her deeply. Joanna felt a joy like none other she had felt in her life, spread through her bones and body. He then looked deeply into her eyes and said, "Well. I'm not the smartest man you will ever know, nor will I ever be the ideal of perfection, but I promise you this Joanna. I am a decent man with a good heart, and I promise to make this life the best we can possibly have together. So, yes. I do want you to stay with me. You're all I've thought about since I met you that day at the library, and you're all I want to think about for the rest of my days." The pair then walked hand in hand into David's modest living room where they sit side by side on the sofa, holding each other until they drifted off peacefully.

ELAINE

TORI BUCKLEMEYER

79

The train screeched to a halt and Elaine Sheldon had to brace herself for the onslaught of people trying to squeeze past out. Holding tightly around the handrail, she winced when a rushing man bumped his laptop bag against her hips, and she took a few steps back with the impact.

The man did not stop to apologize and Elaine only heaved a sigh and fixed her stance as the train resumed moving.

It was supposed to be a five-minute walk from the station to her apartment, but tonight, it did not feel like it. Her steps were slow and her shoulders were drooped. The streetlights refused to turn on properly and it flickered repeatedly as she passed by. Elaine sighed at the dreary atmosphere.

Just a week ago, these walks home passed by with a spring in her step, looking forward to the person who was waiting for her to be back, the person she had been going home to for the past six months, the man who welcomed her with a warm hug and a big smile after a tiring day at work—until the other day.

Her eyes felt heavy and the long wait for the elevator was not helping with her mood. She watched as the red arrow went down as minutes passed by until it reached the ground floor. Her ride back up was spent alone. She smiled bitterly. The world must really hate her.

All doors were closed when she alighted at the twelfth floor except for one. For a second, she almost panicked thinking that the opened door was hers, only to realize that it was the empty unit beside hers. Boxes are stacked in front of the door and the sound of a man's groans can be heard as she came closer.

She battled with herself if she should help or not. As the next-door neighbor, she knew she should, as a sign of welcome for the new occupant, but she also knew that the feeling in her chest is heavier than those boxes. She scoffed at her dramatics but looked down at herself. Her arms were already crying in protest with her handbag and laptop bag and those boxes looked nowhere near light so she forgot being thoughtful for once and unlocked her door. She was about to go inside when a man's voice startled her.

"Hi. Do you live next door?" The man beamed at her but the smile didn't reach his eyes.

Elaine smiled back, a closed-lip one. "And you must be my new neighbor," she offered her hand which the man accepted. "Elaine."

"Ivan. It's nice to meet you," he let go of her hand and gestured at the boxes. "I'll be done in a minute. You don't have to worry about the noises." He smiled again but Elaine can only see a grimace.

"Don't worry, take your time. I would have helped you but—"

Ivan waved his hand no. "No need. You must be tired from work," he observed, noticing the formal attire and the laptop bag hanging on her shoulders. "Go on ahead. Have a good night."

"You too," she returned in a clip tone and sent a brief smile again before going inside. The bang of the door echoed throughout the dark empty unit, reminding Elaine that she had no company anymore, that she had to spend the night alone in her empty apartment.

A tear escaped down her cheeks, which ended with bouts of sobbing for the third consecutive night.

—-

There are things in life that once you get a taste of, you'd never want to let go. And for Elaine, that was her relationship with Christian.

They started dating a little over a year ago, when they met at a mutual friend's party, though neither are close enough to the celebrant and her friends so they ended up chatting the night away. A week later, they found themselves agreeing to date exclusively.

Elaine did not have high hopes with her relationship at the start. Christian seemed to be the happy-go-lucky type of guy who always acted on a whim instead of having plans. She wasn't in too deep yet, so she didn't mind it at all.

But as the months go by and their relationship turned for the better, people around them started to notice—that Christian is changing for the good and it was mainly because of his relationship with Elaine. It flattered the female, she won't deny it. Knowing that she may be one of the reasons why Christian was trying to find a stable job, having the courage to pursue his passion in photography, and planning for his future, made her pleased.

All along, Elaine was expecting that she was included in the plan. It only dawned on her that she was never part of the picture when one day, she got home, expecting the smell of pepperoni and cheese for their usual pizza night, only to find a large bag filled with all of Christian's things that had accumulated in her home. They never agreed to stay together officially but they might as well be for all the days and weekends the male had stayed with her.

At first, she thought he was going for a vacation. She could've accepted it, a six-month out of the country trips to take images of the wonders of nature. What she didn't understand was why he had to break up with her.

They could've made it worked, Elaine believed so. She trusted herself to stay faithful and she put the same amount of trust on Christian. It just so happened that her ex-boyfriend did not believe in long distance relationships. It even hurt more when he said that he's not even sure if he's even coming back. His career was just starting, he said. It could be his one in a lifetime opportunity, he said. All Elaine could do was cry and beg him to at least try, but he was already decided.

And that was it. The end of a year-long relationship in just a snap.

—

The pastor was going through the sermon part and Elaine pinched her forearm to stay focused. They had to work overtime last night and she barely had a wink of sleep before she raced to be on time to the church.

Attending the mass was a weekly thing for Elaine. Christian never accompanied her no matter how much she forced him to and now, she's secretly grateful because at the least, she has this one activity she was used to doing alone.

The pastor's voice resounded against the walls and she snapped back into attention. Someone, a man perhaps judging by the black slacks and the scent, sat beside her. She almost rolled her eyes for the man's tardiness but bit her lips when she realized that she was no better for drifting off instead of listening.

The pastor droned on and she could hear the sound of the piano and the jingle of the tambourine but it faded as her lids became heavier.

By the time she woke up, people were standing up and were walking towards the exit. Elaine jolted in her seat, lifting her head from a sturdy shoulder she was leaning on, cheeks crimsoning due to the embarrassment.

She looked to her right and her eyes widened while the color of her cheeks got redder. "Ivan," she muttered. Of all people to fall asleep on while a mass was ongoing, it had to be her new next-door neighbor.

Ivan chuckled and raised his hand to his lip, which confused Elaine. When it dawned on her, she turned around and wiped the bit of drool that escaped her lips.

Clearing her throat and checking discreetly if there was still drool left, she turned back again to an amused Ivan. At least now, the smile reached his eyes unlike the first time she saw him.

"I'm sorry for falling asleep on you," she pursed her lips. An old lady passing by gave her a stink eye and she refused to shrink on her seat in shame.

Her neighbor saw the gesture and he chuckled. "It's okay. You went home late didn't you?"

"How did you know?" Her eyebrows furrow.

Ivan looked more amused now. "I heard your door. It wasn't exactly hard to when it's the dead hour of the morning," he explained.

Elaine nodded, laughing at herself for thinking of anomalous things such as Ivan being a stalker or a creep. It crossed her mind that it was still strange for him to be awake at such an hour but then that would mean it was also strange for her to have just come home so she didn't bring it up.

"Oh!" She unconsciously glanced over his shoulder and found a tiny, wet mark. Scrambling for tissues, she pulled a handful and wiped at his clothes furiously. "I am so sorry," she apologized repeatedly until Ivan had to hold her hand to stop her.

"It's spit. No big deal. No one's gonna die," he smiled once again. Elaine thought he should smile more often. It brightens up his face. Meanwhile, her face was on fire.

"Can I treat you for coffee then? As sorry and welcome?"

"I'd love to but I have somewhere to be. Maybe next time," he said noncommittally.

"Next time then." She apologized again before racing back home. A loud 'I'm home' is on the tip of her tongue but she stopped herself just in time.

Elaine dragged her feet to the sofa and flopped down unceremoniously with her legs hanging on an arm. Tears cascaded down her temples, which progressed into sobs. Her chest felt tight and her breath was constricted.

Earlier, she prayed to God to give her Christian back. She wished that Christian would change his mind and call her, or at least send her a message, saying sorry and that he wants her back.

She was praying but the pain hurt like hell. She asked God why did this have to happen to her, why she had to feel such pain, why she had to feel hopeful for her future for once, only for it to crumble right in front of her.

It was so unfair. She gave it her all but all she got was nothing.

—-

It had been a month since the breakup and Elaine was faring better. She haven't cried herself to sleep for two weeks now and she even had the energy to go out for a walk. It wasn't much but it was a start. She still thought of her ex-boyfriend from time to time, which was inevitable considering every corner of her apartment reminded her of him, but the pangs were getting less painful. In a way she didn't know how, she was getting by.

It was a Sunday and she was on her way to the church. A friend, Leslie, welcomed her with a hug.

"You're looking great, dear." The shorter female brushed her cheek against Elaine's and Elaine had to chuckle at her affections.

"Hi, how have you been? I haven't seen you here lately?"

Leslie beamed at her in delight. "I went on a vacation with Luis to France. Oh, we have to get some coffee later. I have lots of stories to tell you," she narrated giddily, the smile never wavering off her face.

"How's Christian? Still sleeping I bet?" Leslie chuckled and Elaine's eyes twitched. She swallowed a lump in her throat and an awkward silence passed before her friend realized that something was wrong.

"Hey, what's wrong?"

Elaine cleared her throat and forced a smile. "W-we broke up," she cursed at herself for stuttering. It felt more real every time she had to say it outloud and it doubled the sharp pain that coursed through her.

Leslie looked shocked beyond belief at the news and scrambled to wrap her arms around Elaine again. "I'm so sorry!"

Elaine, who had to fight the tears that were threatening to come out, hugged her back, glad to have someone to comfort her even if it was a month late. "It's okay. It's been a month."

She pulled back and wiped the tears that escaped despite her resistance. "I'm all right," she forced out a smile. Her friend looked at her worriedly but let it go for now. "All right, let's have lunch together okay?" Leslie asked, to which Elaine said yes. It had been a while since she had a meal with another person aside from her co-workers and she welcomed the thought now more than ever.

The mass lasted for a little over an hour and Leslie pulled her to a nearby Italian cafe that served great pasta and gelato. Elaine was grateful for the distraction but she could not help but glance at a table for two at a corner. She mentally sighed and erased the memories in her head.

—-

Elaine was working on a report when a call came. Not expecting anybody, she looked at her phone quizzically, which registered Leslie's name. Leslie rarely contacted her through the phone.

Surprised, she accepted the call and had to brace herself for a joyful Leslie who almost screeched a 'hello.'

"Hey, what's up?" Elaine reclined back on her seat and shut her eyes. She could hear her stomach grumbling only to remember that she didn't eat anything for lunch.

"I know this might be too soon, but it's been two months and it's not too soon right?" She said rapidly and Elaine had to sit up straight again and focus on her words to keep up.

"What exactly might be too soon?"

Leslie paused dramatically. Elaine could almost hear her excitement through the receiver.

"Dating."

"Dating?" Elaine repeated dumbly.

"Yeah, dating. I figure it's about time you meet new people. What do you think?" Elaine processed everything before saying an alarmed 'what' as a reaction.

She sighed before continuing. "Leslie, I know you have the best intentions in mind. But if you still didn't know, I barely have time to meet new people."

"But you have the time," Leslie insisted. "Every Sundays. Don't you always save your Sundays?"

"I do. But that's for church and some me time. I don't feel like going to a party or anything after a mass."

"Exactly. For church. And forget the me time, you have more than enough of that," Leslie paused and apologized for the insensitive remark, which Elaine only waved away. Leslie was just telling the truth.

"What I actually wanted to say is that I know this guy, from the church we go to, who you might be interested to meet," Leslie drawled on. It took a minute before it registered what she was suggesting.

"Are you setting me up on a blind date?" She asked incredulously.

"Uh, yes," her friend admitted sheepishly.

Elaine rubbed a thumb on a temple. "Do I have a say on this?"

"Not really. I already set up the time and date."

"Leslie—!"

"I had to! I know you're gonna say no!"

"Whatever. Just text me the details. I have work to do," Elaine grumbled. She heard a faint 'I love you' before she hung up the phone and she felt a little bad for not saying it back to her dear friend.

—-

That night, Elaine turned and tossed on her bed. She couldn't stop thinking about the blind date and she had bombarded herself with too much questions that only left her more confused and doubtful.

Is it too soon? What if Christian knows about it? What if the guy isn't what she's expecting him to be? But then, what exactly are her expectations?

The fact that he goes to her church is a good point, but the thought that she saw it as a good point gnaws at her guilt. It might be ridiculous but she felt guilty for indirectly saying yes to the blind date. It had been two months but thinking of a possibility of a relationship with anyone other than Christian brought a bad taste to her mouth.

—-

Elaine pushed the glass door open before a waitress assisted her to her seat. A man was already seated at the table, but she could not see his face yet.

A gasp escaped her lips when the waitress stopped and gestured at their table, making the man look up.

"Elaine?" Ivan said, sounding shell-shocked himself.

"You're Leslie's friend?" Elaine asked for good measure. She had not seen her neighbor for weeks now. The last time, they only exchanged brief hellos when they happened to meet while taking out trash.

Ivan stood up and helped her pull her seat back, before returning to his own side.

"And you are Leslie's friend," Ivan jokingly deadpanned. Elaine took her seat and began to chuckle. Ivan, amused by the situation, also began to laugh.

"I guess we'll be having a date today?" He asked with a smile on his face. Elaine hummed in affirmation while smiling from ear to ear.

"How did you meet Leslie?" Elaine asked once their food was served.

"I actually knew Luis first. He was an old friend and he was the one who suggested this place for me to move to," Ivan explained before taking a bite of the grilled chicken.

Elaine took a sip of water before responding. "Why did you move? Was it for your job?"

The question froze Ivan for a second before he relaxed. Elaine bit her tongue for the question which obviously hit a nerve.

"You don't have to answer it if you don't want to," She said softly.

"Sorry," he offered a timid smile.

"It's okay," she smiled before diverting the conversation to a different topic.

It turned out that they have a lot of similar interests than they could have expected. They have the same fascination with the Harry Potter series, the same geeky side when it came to Star Wars, and the same passion when it came to football—though Elaine loved Man U with a passion while Ivan preferred Chelsea.

Hours later, they found themselves laughing comfortably around each other while they walk together home. They stopped when they reached Elaine's door and Ivan kept a good distance, to which Elaine was grateful for.

"I really had a lot of fun," Ivan smiled.

"Me too. I think it's been ages since I've laughed that much," Elaine gushed.

He put his hands in his pant's back pockets and Elaine mentally chuckled.

"We should do this again some other time?" It was more of a question rather than a statement.

Elaine let out a deep breath she didn't know she had been holding and nodded. "Sure."

—-

She threw the frame inside the black plastic bag and flinched at the sound of breaking glass. Next were the t-shirts and boxers that were definitely not hers, followed by other toilet utilities that were never meant for a woman.

It was a day after her blind date and last night, she had the urge to throw away everything that reminded her of Christian. It had been months but she still kept some of his belongings that he left there, silently holding on to the hope that he would come back.

This move did not mean anything but a sign of her trying to move on. She had been meaning to do it for weeks but the date with Ivan was the last push she needed to start working on it. She sniffed and sobbed for the first few minutes but it got better as the plastic bag got fuller.

It was filled with pictures, letters, dried flowers, candy and chocolate wrappers, and almost every single thing that Christian gave her during their relationship, including the bracelet that he gifted to her last Christmas. It took a lot of emotional effort but afterwards, she felt lighter, as if an invisible baggage was thrown away.

The door next to her opened just as she was pulling the plastic bag outside to throw it in the bin. Ivan looked as surprised as she was. He was sporting a shirt paired with loose shorts and running shoes.

"Going for a run at night?" She asked, eyeing his outfit.

Ivan shrugged. "The park's good enough for some laps."

Elaine stopped for a second to think before taking a leap of faith. "Mind if I join you?"

—

The night was a bit chilly but fortunately, there was minimal wind.

Elaine had been living in that neighborhood for years but it was the first time that she jogged at the park. She always thought it was full of rowdy teenagers getting drunk or creeps who had nothing better to do with their lives. Ivan laughed at her when she voiced it out.

"This place's actually good," He panted, arms swinging as they jogged around the vicinity. "You should just avoid Friday nights because it can be too crowded."

She looked at him curiously. "How long have you been going here?" She asked, breaths coming short. Ivan slowed his pace a bit.

"Since the first week I moved," he answers. "It was a bit lonely staying indoors."

Elaine stopped in her tracks, causing Ivan to stop too.

"I am so sorry for being a very unwelcoming neighbor. I should have made you something and came over to check on you."

Ivan rested a hand on her head and ruffled her hair. Elaine felt like pulling away but didn't, surprised at how large his hand felt. "No need to feel sorry. I know it wasn't your best day then," he continued jogging and she followed automatically.

She gulped as she remembered that day. It was definitely one of her most miserable days. "Yeah. My boyfriend just broke up with me a few days before that," she chuckled dryly. This time, it was Ivan who stopped first.

"I am so sorry to hear that."

She pursed her lips in thought. "It's okay. I've been doing great. It wasn't an excuse to not welcome you," she patted his shoulder, signaling him to continue moving.

It was silent for a few minutes before Ivan spoke up again.

"I just got divorced a few months ago."

Elaine screeched to a halt. "What?" Her eyes widen at her rude reaction. "I mean, when?"

"A few weeks before I moved," Ivan looked down. "My ex-wife and I just got divorced and I realized I can't stay at our home for long so I sold it, and moved here," he gestured at his surroundings with feigned enthusiasm. "And I think I made a great decision."

Elaine took a step closer before wrapping her arms around him. "I am sorry to hear that."

She could feel him shaking his head as he hugged her back. "I guess we're both sorry to hear about each other's heartbreaks?" he joked to lighten the mood. She pushed him back and hit him lightly on the chest before laughing.

They both broke into fits of laughter, earning the questioning looks of the passers-by.

—

They continued to contact each other throughout the week. They may be neighbors but Elaine frequently opted to work until late night so they can't really meet much. Leslie called once to check on how the date went and squealed when Elaine responded with a simple 'Thank you' and shouted 'I knew it, I knew it' repeatedly until it burned Elaine's ears.

The following Sunday, Elaine and Ivan agreed to go to the church together, causing Leslie to get excited upon seeing them.

She looked at them knowingly and winked at Elaine, who blushed at her friend's action. Ivan chuckled at the sight but pretended that he did not see it. All of them, including Luis, Leslie's boyfriend, sat side-by-side inside the church.

During the mass, Elaine prayed and asked for guidance, if what she was doing was right or if it was too soon to consider liking a different man. When she opened her eyes and looked at Ivan's direction, she found him to be staring back at her.

She glanced away and fought down the blush that crept on her cheeks.

—

It was a Wednesday night and usually, Elaine would still be at work, doing things that were not really urgent.

When she got home, it was way too early for bedtime and she found herself thinking of the man living in the unit beside hers. Curiously, she laid an ear flat on the surface of the wall to check for any noises. She didn't know why but she wanted to check if Ivan was home.

She could hear a faint sound of music and she thought about it once, twice, and multiple times before deciding to send him a message.

A few minutes later, there were knocks on her door. Elaine, already clad in more comfortable clothes, welcomed the sight of Ivan carrying chips and soda.

"Did you bring any DVDs?" She helped him bring the things to her living room and settled them on the coffee table. Ivan reached for his back and pulled out some cases and handed them to her.

She raised her eyebrows at the choices. "So you're basically suggesting we watch the whole series of Harry Potter?" She looked at him pointedly.

Ivan shrugged before making himself comfortable on the couch. "Pretty much," he grinned.

In the middle of the movie, they found themselves sitting close to each other, shoulders almost bumping. Elaine looked at her side and it was only a few inches away from Ivan's. Unconsciously, she continued to stare until he looked back.

"Like what you see?" he grinned mischievously, earning a smack on his chest.

"Your scar," she started, pertaining to a small scar at the left corner of his lips.

"Ah, they're battle scars," he jested. Her forehead scrunched at the vague answer.

Ivan sighed before reclining fully. "I had a bit of a scuffle last year. I saw my then wife with another man and I confronted them right on the spot. And the rest is history," he smiled but the bitterness was pronounced.

Elaine copied his position and leaned her head on his shoulder. It was a bold move and she was holding her breath if the male would shrug her off. However, Ivan lifted his arm and rested it on her shoulder so she could scoop closer. Elaine let the tension seep out of her body.

"I only have one question," she said after a while.

"What is it?" He closed his eyes, hoping that he could answer it whatever the question was.

"He got it worse right? I mean, you managed to hit his face at least twice? With bruises?"

Ivan burst out laughing. "Yes, yes, I did. I kicked him in the stomach, too. It was pretty satisfying," he answered, still chuckling at the unexpected question.

"Good," She said before placing an arm over his stomach.

They watched the rest of the movies in the same position.

—-

Elaine was typing her report when her boss approached her.

"I read your latest report, about the success rate if the company decides to venture in e-commerce." She waited with bated breath. It was a report she had been working extra hard for.

"And I can say I'm impressed. I sent a copy to the higher-ups and we just have to wait for their comments," he patted her on the shoulder.

Elaine beamed and said thank you.

"You should continue doing what you've been doing recently," he commented, puzzling Elaine.

"I mean, you look happier. Whatever the reason is, continue doing it," he said before turning back to his office.

Elaine could only think of one big change in her life recently. Biting her lips to stop herself from grinning too widely, she smiled at the thought of a man.

—

She was preparing the TV and the player for their usual movie night when Ivan received a call. His expression dimmed and his jaw locked when he saw who was calling but still answered it, walking towards the kitchen for some privacy.

Elaine, though worried, stayed where she was and fiddled with her own phone. She tried to give Ivan the privacy he needed but was surprised when his voice got louder.

"I don't give a fuck about it. I'm deleting your number. Please don't call me anymore."

She could hear the sound of a phone hitting the floor and she scrambled off the sofa to check on him.

Ivan was staring at the broken device and his chest was heaving deeply. Slowly, she walked towards him and reached for his shoulders. He relaxed at the touch and rubbed a hand on his face.

"I'm sorry you have to hear that," he reached for her hand and pulled her closer to him before hugging her waist.

Elaine put her hand on his hair and carded her fingers through the black strands.

"It was my ex-wife," he explained, making Elaine halt her actions for a moment. She only resumed when Ivan nudged her hand with his head. "She was telling me about her wedding in two weeks, and that I'm invited." He laughed bitterly. "She cheated on me and she had the guts to invite me to her wedding."

Elaine, now shaken, fought the tears that are threatening to spill. She can feel the hurt from Ivan's voice and it was affecting her more than it should.

She remained silent, listening to Ivan's breath until he completely relaxed and his breaths evened out.

The silence was deafening until Elaine had the courage to break it. "Do you still love her?"

It was a yes-no question but Ivan didn't respond for the next two seconds, nor even for the next minutes.

Feeling defeated, Elaine pulled herself from his grasp, ignoring his pleas to make her stay. She collected her things from his living room before walking her way outside and into her own unit. Ivan knocked on her door for a few minutes until she said from the other side.

"Please. Stop it. I need some time alone."

The knocks stopped, and a few seconds later, another door was shut.

—-

Just months ago, it was Christian who was the cause of Elaine's sleepless nights. It was him who was the reason why she cried and continuously asked herself of what's wrong with her and why do people find it so hard to love her. It was him who was the reason why she didn't want to wake up to face another day and tempted her to just laze on her bed, feeling as if all the energy had been sucked out from her.

But now, just a few months later, Ivan had been occupying her mind much more than she expected he would.

He is a good man. He's nice, funny, responsible, smart, and even good-looking—a complete catch if she dared say. When she first saw him, all sweaty and panting from carrying heavy boxes, she just saw him as just another attractive man who happened to be her neighbor and nothing else. Admittedly, she even forgot about him until their embarrassing encounter at the church. That was how it was, but because of one date, it turned into something more.

Elaine found herself genuinely enjoying Ivan's company as they spent more time together. It started from scheduled dates and movie nights until they found themselves into a routine of being together every other day, whether it was to just talk, share about their day, or watch movies.

It was a routine that they easily adapted too—they never forced themselves into it nor did they set fixed days and to-do lists whenever they meet. Day by day, Elaine found herself thinking of her ex-boyfriend less, and whenever she did, it was to smile at the memories they shared and never to wallow in the sadness and the gaping hole he made when he left.

As Ivan made her feel light-hearted, carefree and secured, she found herself forgetting about the heartbreaking nights, about the times when she went back to an empty home, and about the thrown away pictures and gifts. With Ivan, she felt that she could try again, that she could, maybe, fall in love again.

But it seemed that Ivan thought otherwise. She could still see how hurt he was when he talked about his ex-wife inviting him to her wedding. She could remember how tightly clenched his fists were and how much he was trembling in anger. It was a sight she never expected to see from the usually composed man.

When she asked that question she wasn't hoping for an absolute no. They were married and she knew that he must have felt so strongly for her to ask for her hand. But at the least, she was expecting something along the lines of 'I'm doing fine' or 'I'm getting over it' and it would have sufficed, for her at least.

If anything, it made her realize how much she was wearing her heart on her sleeve yet again. She wasn't in love with him, not yet at least, but she knew she was on her way. All along, she thought he felt the same, that he was moving forward and trying to forget his past heartbreak, just like her. Elaine thought that a part of him had thought about her in a romantic way, that she might be someone who he can ideally like, but then again, those were just Elaine's assumptions.

The problem with her, as always, were her hopes and baseless assumptions. These always manage to fuck her emotionally—big time. She just never learned.

—

Ivan tried to contact her in the following days but she was resolved on avoiding him for a few days. She was aware that she was being immature but she deemed herself unprepared.

Every day, she recited every line she could say once they managed to talk. She imagined different scenarios and how she would react to them and what she should say. She admitted, most of her though-of situations were bad. She wasn't too hopeful that they would be returning back to the friendly yet flirty camaraderie they had formed.

Elaine was far from being level-headed. When it came to feelings, she was like an open book. She never tried to hide what she was feeling nor did she ever lie about it. So when one day, while standing on the train, hand clasped tightly on the handrail, and a man stood behind her and asked "Will you be my girlfriend?" she broke down in tears and attracted the attention of other commuters.

Among all the scenarios she imagined in her head, this wasn't how it was supposed to be. He wasn't supposed to show out of nowhere and tell her things she has been wishing to hear for weeks in the middle of a crowded train. She tried to stop her tears but the various emotions overwhelmed her.

Ivan had panicked, wiping away her tears furiously with his fingers and then the sleeves of his sweater. He was expecting her to shriek or push him away or to give him the finger, but this wasn't in his imagined reactions.

When the train stopped at the next station, he gently guided Elaine out and continued hushing her. Her cries were now reduced to sobs and Ivan cursed at himself for making her cry.

Once she was calm, she smacked him hardly on his chest, before saying a garbled "Yes."

For a while, Ivan was confused why she said that but broke into a large grin when he realized the implication.

Overjoyed, he grabbed her face with both hands and kissed her, right in the middle of the station, with some bystanders looking away from the scene. The kiss was chaste yet sweet. Their lips glided smoothly against each other and for a while, Ivan was tempted to press harder, which was futile when Elaine pushed him.

"But," Elaine sniffed and shushed him with a finger on his lips. "Explain."

"Could I take you home first? It's starting to get cold," he gestured at her working clothes—a thin blouse and a pencil skirt—and led them outside and hailed a cab.

There was a deafening silence throughout the ride home and their way up in the elevator, but Ivan never let go of her hand the whole time.

He led them to his unit instead of Elaine's and she was about to protest but he insisted.

He pushed her until she was seated on the sofa and he sat beside her as closely as possible. She squirmed in her seat and he gave her some space, rubbing his neck sheepishly.

He reached for her hand and turned his body towards her.

He started with a deep breath before launching to his long narrative. "That night, when you asked me if I still loved her, I was sure that my answer was no," He brought a hand up when he saw that she was about to interrupt him.

He continued once she silently agrees to keep on listening.

"But at the same time, I can't say it. It sounds more real once you say it out loud doesn't it? Am I making any sense?" He chuckled. Meanwhile, Elaine responded that yes, she understands because she felt the same thing with Christian.

"We were a couple since high school, and then through college. Most people called us the ideal couple and were just waiting for us to get married. It was as if there was no other way out of it but to build our own family. So I did ask for her hand in marriage and she said yes." Ivan heaved a deep breath, composing his next words in his mind.

"But as soon as we started living together, something felt...weird. A year later, I realized how used we are to being together. We were so used to seeing each other, to doing things together that it only seemed natural that we got married. I realized that maybe, we took marriage for granted, and it was a hurried decision merely out of obligation because of the people's expectations."

"We started to drift away from each other then. In the back of my mind, I knew she was thinking the same thing. When I saw her with another man, it hurt me—not because I still love her but because I was at least expecting that we wouldn't reach that point where we would hide secrets behind each other's backs—especially a lover at that."

"I saw red and then I found myself furious. I was angry at her but more at myself for letting us be trapped in that situation. When we decided on the divorce, it was heartbreaking but it felt like a burden

I never knew I had was lifted from me. It felt liberating." He paused, tightening his hold on Elaine's hand. Elaine returned the gesture, egging him to go on.

"I admit. It still hurts. But not because I still love her but more from the fact that I spent so many years thinking I was happy but realized that I wasn't. It was hard coming to terms with that: that I forced myself to think that everything was alright when it wasn't. And then suddenly, she told me the news that she's getting married and practically screaming at me that she's found her happiness. I'm happy for her. We've been together for so long that I can't even bear thinking of hating her. But then I thought of myself and my sorry state of a coward who can't even ask you to be mine and I was enraged because I felt that it was unfair. I thought that I deserve my own happiness too." His voice trembled then and he blinked repeatedly as his eyes began to get misty.

Elaine knelt beside him and pulled his head to her chest, rubbing his back consolingly at the confession.

"I'm sorry if I hurt you. Because all these just came crashing on me and I suddenly couldn't answer. I didn't know where to start. It felt too much." She felt a wetness on her arm and hugged him more tightly. If she could only take a part of the pain he was feeling, she would do it.

"I'm sorry for assuming the worst, and for not giving you a chance to explain." She muttered, kissing a spot in his head to reassure him that she was there, and she won't be leaving anytime soon.

Ivan retreated and pulled her into his lap, resting his forehead against hers. "I'm sorry for giving you the chance to assume the worst, then. If anything, I just really want to say how much I like you and how much you make me happy." He gave her a peck and kept his lips there, feeling the smile forming on his lips.

"I'm really glad I met you. I'd do anything I could so you could forget him completely."

Elaine shook her head no in protest. "No, Ivan. We will work together so we could heal completely. This is no you helping me, nor me helping you. This is us helping each other," she said, gazing into his eyes lovingly.

He smiled a smile that reached his eyes, the one that Elaine absolutely adored, before replying. "I love the sound of that."

END

Amish Innocence

MONICA MARKS

Lavina gasped and whirled, startled at the door slammed against the barn wall. Her hand flew to her throat as if to steady her heartrate.

"Lizzie!" she breathed at her sister. "You must be more careful with the door!"

Elizabeth Blauch grinned sheepishly and looked at the swinging wood.

"Sorry, Lavvy. I always forget how temperamental it can be."

She smiled at the abashed girl as her pulse regained normalcy.

"It has been this way for as long as we have been on this earth," she replied, laughing.

"More the reason I would always imagined it would have been fixed by now!" Elizabeth retorted.

Lavina stepped out of the stable, placing the broom against the door. She dusted off her hands on a simple white apron before returning her attention to her sister.

"Are you looking for me?" she asked, securing the empty stall and Lizzie looked uncomfortable.

"Yes…"

Lavina waited, staring expectantly at Elizabeth to finish but the girl seemed unwilling to speak.

"Are we playing a guessing game, Lizzie?"

"I wanted to tell you that Eli came calling," Elizabeth blurted out.

She whirled to face her sister, her brown eyes narrowing in annoyance.

"What could he possibly want this time?" she growled and Elizabeth sighed.

"He left a note," she replied, handing a folded piece of paper to her. The older sister shook her auburn head and scowled at the message.

"Use it in the wood stove," she snapped. "He has nothing to say that I want to hear."

Lizzie nodded in agreement, ripping the letter in two pieces.

"You are so strong, Lavina. Another woman would have fallen to pieces after what he did to you."

Lavina did not respond and the two walked from the barn where the older sister had spent the afternoon cleaning.

She did not hear me sobbing into my pillow at night afterward, she thought, glancing at Lizzie out of her peripheral vision. Lizzie skipped along lightly and Lavina was overcome by a fusion of affection and shame.

She adored her sisters. Lizzie was the second youngest and Lavina the second oldest. They were very close both in age and in spirit and Lavina shared most of her thoughts with the high spirited younger girl.

Most of them. If she knew everything, she would be so hurt.

Lizzie's abrupt appearance in the stables had shocked her but not because of the unruly barn door. Lavina had been lost in thought, thoughts she had no business thinking.

Guilt and consternation had swept through her as she stared at her sister as if Lizzie was able to see what she was planning.

What am I planning? Lavina asked herself grouchily. *You have yet to figure that out for yourself.*

"Lavvy, have you heard a word I spoke?"

More humiliation flooded through the older sibling and her pale skin turned crimson. Lizzie immediately saw the heat in her cheeks.

"Why are you blushing?"

Lavina turned her head as they approached the house.

"It is hot today," she fibbed, the words leaving a strange taste in her mouth. She was unaccustomed to lying, especially to her family. Lizzie continued to stare at her.

"It is not that hot," Lizzie muttered, opening the side door to allow Lavina inside but the lovely redhaired girl shook her head.

"No, I have work to do in the garden yet," she told her sister. Lizzie threw her hands up in exasperation, her own coffee colored eyes darkening with suspicion.

"Lavina, are you certain you are alright?"

The older sister nodded quickly, offering her sister a tight smile.

"Yes, of course."

"It is almost time for supper. The garden can wait until tomorrow," Lavina told her. As she opened her mouth to argue, Elizabeth spoke again.

"I suspect that Eli might return."

Lavina gritted her teeth.

"He will not if he knows what is good for him," she grumbled but she glanced at Lizzie's concerned face and relented.

"Yes, you are right," she agreed, sighing. She did wish to be caught alone with Eli that afternoon or any other for that matter. It was bad enough she was forced to see him in the community and at worship.

He should not be coming around. I will have Daed talk to his father or the deacon. This is becoming harassment.

Lavina did not wish to go that route for it would arouse a lot of questions she did not wish to answer and shine a negative light on Eli. It went against the bronze haired beauty's gentle way to create ripples. She hoped that her ex-boyfriend's fixation on her would falter but she suspected that he was only getting started.

It is not me whom he wants; he is simply angered that I caught onto his sneaky, despicable ways and he could not talk his way out of them. He thinks he can woo me back with his charm but I am wise to who he is now. I will never go back, no matter how many letters he leaves or flowers he sends.

In a way, Lavina was grateful having discovered Eli's girlfriend in a neighboring district. She had no idea how he thought he would have gotten away with such a cunning deception but he had managed throughout their entire six-month courtship while Lavina patiently waited for a marriage proposal.

It was not until the other woman had grown distrustful of Eli's comings and goings that she surprised him at worship one Sunday morning and Eli had found himself caught.

To the girl's credit, she had not caused a scene, quietly wishing him and Lavina good luck before retreating in her wagon to her own district. Lavina had then been faced with a difficult choice; forgiveness or turn her back on the man she had been certain she was going to marry.

"If he could do such a brazenly disrespectful thing to you for half a year, Lavvy, he is hardly the wagon which you would want to hitch your horse to," Lizzie had told her and Lavina knew her sister was right.

It was at that time that Lavina began to question her desire to stay in the Amish community.

The Ordnung is meant to keep us humble and free of the influences and desires which outsiders enshroud themselves, Lavina thought sadly. *But there is no more security here than there is beyond here. We are secluded to be protected and together but we can be just as alienated and alone as anywhere else.*

Lavina had been baptized the year before, her faith unwavering before the blow she had been delivered by Eli's infidelity. She had never wanted a life beyond the sanctuary of the one she had known in Holmes County. Yet almost overnight, something had changed within her. Eli had created a distrust in her and a yearning to escape. While she had not spoken of Eli's cruelty to anyone, she could not shake the sense that people were talking about her. Lavina felt eyes on her everywhere she went.

She had decided that she would not stand for it any longer.

"Lavina, you are beginning to concern me," Lizzie told her quietly and she realized she had once more drifted off in thought.

"I apologize," she told her sister. "I was just pondering why that man will not leave well enough alone."

"You should go directly to his parents and tell them what kind of boy they have raised," Lizzie announced as they washed their hands. Rebecca looked up from the island in the kitchen where she was chopping vegetables.

"Are you speaking of Eli?" she asked and Lizzie nodded. The middle sister sighed inwardly. She was truly not in the mood to discuss her ex.

"What he did is reproachful. Someone should put him in his proper place. Lavvy, have you spoken with the deacon about this atrocity?"

"No, she has not spoken to anyone!" Lizzie sighed with annoyance.

"And I wish you would stop speaking of it also," Lavina snapped. Her sisters stared at her in surprise. The gentle redhead did not often raise her voice.

"We are concerned for you," Rebecca told her, turning back to the task on the counter but Lavina could read the hurt in her expression.

"I know you are but I would much rather forget the entire sordid affair," she said softly, wishing to strike the stricken look from her sister's face.

An awkward silence ensued.

"What else needs to be done?" Lavina asked Rebecca, indicating the dinner preparation but she shook her dark hair.

"Nothing. We are having a visitor for supper," she said in a clipped tone and Lavina knew that Rebecca wanted to brood alone. Rebecca was the least forgiving of the four siblings, apt to long bouts of sulking when her feelings were hurt.

"Who is coming?" Lizzie asked. Rebecca's brown eyes flashed.

"I do not know! An outsider."

Elizabeth and Lavina stared at one another in surprise but they knew pushing Rebecca for more information would be futile. Her mood was already ruined.

"I will be in my room," Lavina announced and her younger sister tried to follow her but she stopped Lizzie at the threshold.

"I would like to lay down for a moment before supper," she told her sister. An expression of hurt crossed over Lizzie's face but she nodded begrudgingly.

"Are you feeling unwell?"

"My head is hurting," Lavina answered truthfully. "I may have been in the sun too long without water today."

"Shall I get you something to drink?"

Shame sparked through the older sister again.

You have a family who loves you dearly. How can you be considering such an atrocious act? You will disrupt their lives with your own selfishness.

"Yes, that would be lovely, Lizzie."

Elizabeth's rosebud mouth curved into a happy smile and she turned to run back down the stairs, eager to help.

Quickly, Lavina slipped into her room and dropped to her knees at her bed. Glancing furtively at the closed door, she dug around under the mattress, her hand closing around a piece of paper at the center of the twin bed and pulled it out.

She had read it many times in the past month but it did not deter her from scanning it again.

This is the paper which will give me options in the English world. Without it, I will not stand a chance.

She heard her sister climbing the wood stairs and Lavina carefully replaced the document back in its hiding spot, jumping onto the bed. A second later, Elizabeth entered with a glass of water.

"You will never guess who *Daed* invited to supper," her younger sister gushed, thrusting the water to Lavina in excitement. She redhead accepted it and took a dutiful sip, trying to seem interested. Obviously, Elizabeth had pressed Rebecca for more details when she went downstairs.

"Who?" she asked.

"An Englisher!"

Lavina felt her heart speed up. It was not unusual for their father to invite outsiders for supper. Not only was Elmo Blauch a skilled furniture maker in the community doing business with the English daily, he was also a minister. People from all walks of life found themselves in their humble dining room breaking bread.

Yet that day, the word "Englisher" sent a fission of alarm coursing through Lavina as if whomever was coming was about to decide which course which she was going to embark upon.

"Why is this news?" Lavina asked nonchalantly, averting her dark eyes toward the bed nervously.

"He is trying to become Amish!" Lizzie declared gleefully. Lavina's eyes jumped to her sister's face to gage if she was joking.

"*He is trying to become Amish?*" she echoed. "I did not realize the church allowed for such things to happen."

Elizabeth shrugged.

"I did not either but according to Rebecca, this man has been in the district for one week already."

"Where is he staying?" Suddenly Lavina was fascinated.

I wonder what would instill such a sudden desire in someone. Has he no family? No one he will miss if he adopts our way of life?

"He has been living with Mary and Jacob Umble."

"How unusual," Lavina mumbled and her sister nodded in agreement.

"I will leave you to rest but supper will be ready soon," she said, turning for the door. She paused to toss a smile back at Lavina.

"I would offer to bring yours here but I suspect you do not wish to miss this."

"No," Lavina conceded. "I will be there for certain."

She watched as Elizabeth closed the door to the bedroom she shared with Rebecca and listened for her light footsteps to continue out of earshot.

How interesting. Perhaps Gott is giving me a sign. He is sending someone here to take my place when I leave.

Again, Lavina's eyes shifted to the mattress and she thought of the paper under her frame.

I took a big risk obtaining my General Education Diploma without the knowledge of my family. I am fortunate I was not caught but without it, I will be unable to secure a future outside of the community. When the time is right, I will bid good bye to my family and move to the city to start a new life, away from the Amish and away from Eli Smucker.

When Ruby Plank had appeared at worship that fateful Sunday, quietly confronting Eli in her presence, Lavina had wanted to run away and hide forever. Her sisters had been told about his indiscretion and sworn to secrecy but Lavina could not shake the sense of feeling smothered by the community.

If I leave, I will never be welcomed back, not when I have already committed myself to Gott and the Ordnung. I must be sure I am well prepared to go and leave behind everyone.

Immediately, Lavina had enrolled in adult classes at the Holmes Community Center, determined to acquire her GED. She had secretly been fashioning English clothing to wear, slowly gathering a bag which she could take when the moment was right. It was filled with necessities like money, toiletries and snacks.

What else do you need? You are ready to go, she told herself. Lavina knew what she needed; assurance that she was doing the right thing.

As she trudged down the stairs to meet the family for supper, she wondered if she was simply growing cowardly.

You have had your GED for a month, sneaking about like a thief in the night to get it and now you are sitting on your hands as if you have lost your nerve. You must go. You can tell everyone tomorrow and leave on Friday morning. It is time. Eli will continue to be a constant reminder of his own betrayal and you will not feel peace until you are away from him.

"Lavina, are you going to join us or do you intend to eat from the doorway?" Her mother demanded, laughing and Lavina realized she had stopped in the doorway. She flashed her already seated family a brief smile which faded as she saw the stranger in their midst. She lowered her eyes and shuffled toward the table.

"I was laying down," she mumbled, taking her seat.

"If you are unwell, Lavvy, you may take your supper in your room," Belinda Blauch told her daughter but Lavina shook her head.

"No, *Mammi,* I am fine to have supper at the table."

She nodded at the man who sat wedged between her father and Rebecca.

"Adam Everly, this is our fourth daughter, Lavina. Lavina, Adam is new to the community," Elmo announced. Adam stared at her with solemn blue eyes and she felt her heart momentarily ceased to beat. It was not so much an electricity but an undercurrent of sadness she felt from him. It pulsated across the table and filled Lavina with a melancholy she had never felt.

Lavina smiled tightly.

"Welcome, Adam."

"Hannah, will you lead prayer please?" Elmo asked his youngest daughter. Hannah lowered her auburn head and the family followed suit but Lavina found herself eyeing the newcomer covertly.

He was pleasantly attractive with dark blonde hair and rugged features but Lavina could see a stress in his face, a gaunt tightness.

Hannah finished and the family reached for the generous meal placed about the table.

"Where do you hail from, Adam?" Elizabeth asked eagerly. She wasted no time tracking the truth about the man. Rebecca scowled but Lavina could see her listening for a response as she chewed.

"Toledo," Adam replied quickly. Hannah peered at him quizzically and then about the table.

"Oh, I misunderstood," she said, swallowing a forkful of vegetables. "I thought our father was saying you are living in the district."

She seemed confused and Lavina understood why; Adam was dressed as an Amish man. He wore a simple white shirt, suspenders and black, homespun pants.

Elmo cleared his throat and glanced furtively at his wife.

"Adam is looking to convert to our way of life," Elmo replied. Hannah's mouth dropped open in shock but she quickly regained her composure.

"Oh! Oh...well...welcome..." she trailed off lamely, looking to her sisters for assistance. Rebecca and Elizabeth stared at their plates but Lavina could not help herself from staring at the stranger who seemed just as uncomfortable as her youngest sister.

"How are you enjoying our way of life so far?" Lavina heard herself asking. "Surely you must be missing the city and its luxuries by now."

Adam met her gaze and Lavina read defiance but he seemed to relax as he understood she was genuinely asking him and not mocking his choice.

"No," he answered simply. "I do not miss anything about the city."

"Adam has given himself one month to learn our traditions and a basic comprehension of Pennsylvania German," Elmo told his family, smiling fondly at he man.

"That is a steep timeline, Adam," Belinda protested. "There is much to learn."

"I am able to do this," Adam assured her. "If I can find the proper instructors, I am certain I can meet this target date."

"May I ask why the rush?" Lavina heard herself question.

Why do you care? Lavina wished she had the good sense to stop speaking. *You have enough to worry about without getting involved with this outsider's business.*

A shadow crossed over Elmo's face and before Adam could respond he spoke.

"Adam is ambitious. That is a virtuous quality in a man," the minister replied.

"I thought patience was a virtue," Elizabeth chimed and Belinda gave her daughter a reproving look.

"I find his determination refreshing," Elmo told his family meaningfully. "And I wish to help his fulfill his quest. This is why I have enlisted Lavina to help him."

The family stared at him in shock, no one less so than his second born. When she regained her composure, she immediately protested.

"*Daed*, I have chores to attend – "

"There is nothing which demands your specific presence. Rebecca, Lizzie and Hannah can help where needed. Adam has already been in Holmes County for a week which means he is a week behind his goal already. You will teach him the ways of the Amish, Lavina."

Lavina found herself staring balefully at the newcomer who had the decency to appear shamed.

"*Dat*, surely a man would be a better teacher than me. Perhaps you can – "

"Lavina, if I had time, I would happily take Adam under my wing and guide him. Your mother and I are consumed with the store and I also have my duties as minister which to attend. Rebecca must oversee the farm. I am asking you to help a member of your community."

He is not a member of our community! He is an outsider who knows nothing of our ways and who is ruining my plans of leaving.

Everyone stared at Lavina, waiting for a response. She had no choice.

"Tomorrow morning, then, Adam?" she replied, trying to keep the acid from her voice. He nodded gratefully and the family exhaled collectively.

Three weeks is not a terribly long period. I will teach this man what I can and then I will tell my family I am leaving.

Lavina would not admit to herself that she was slightly relieved at the unexpected turn of events. She had not been looking forward to the backlash which her announcement would cause and her father had inadvertently afforded her more time.

It will give me a chance to choose the proper words and soften the hit with everyone, Lavina thought as she rode toward the Umble farm.

Approaching, she saw that Adam was already hard at work on the front porch, painting.

"You are early to rise," she commented, stepping down from the wagon. Adam rose from where he was painting the spindles and smiled briefly.

"I started this yesterday and tried to get it finished before going to your house but I didn't have a chance. I didn't want Mr. and Mrs. Umble to stare at a half-painted patio all day."

"Mary and Jacob," Lavina corrected. Adam stared at her uncomprehendingly.

"Pardon?"

"You should refer to them as Mary and Jacob. We do not use terms like mister and missus. We do not formalize."

Adam looked crushed by the lesson and Lavina smiled to take the seemingly harsh connotation from her words.

"It is different than your custom, I know but our way is one of simplicity. We do not overcomplicate our lives with titles."

"I have been calling them mister and missus for a week," he confessed. "And they did not say a word."

"They did not want to embarrass you but I am here to guide you in our ways and customs so forgive me if I do not hold back. It is not meant to undermine, only instruct."

Adam shook his head, his sky-blue eyes wide with gratitude.

"No, no thank you! I appreciate it!"

"Thank you is another term we use extremely sparingly."

Adam stared at her.

"You aren't serious."

"I am. We are perpetually in a state of thankfulness. It does not need to be expressed continuously."

"I am out of my element here," Adam muttered to himself and Lavina laughed.

"Think of this as moving to another country. You would need to learn the way of life anywhere you went if you wished to assimilate well. This is no different."

Adam nodded slowly.

"Well, now that we have conquered etiquette, where should we go?"

"I thought you might want a driving lesson. Have you handled a wagon before?"

Adam glanced at the cart and laughed.

"It looks pretty straightforward," he said and Lavina nodded seriously.

"Excellent. You may drive then."

The pair stepped toward the cart and Lavina watched as Adam struggled to climb onto the wagon. She smothered a smile.

This will be entertaining, she thought and she was not disappointed. As she climbed in beside him, she observed as he took the reins, pulling back too hard. The horse whinnied and turned to glare at him and Lavina could not help but laugh aloud. Adam cast her a sidelong look and hung his head.

"Okay, maybe it is not as straightforward as I initially thought," he said, handing her the straps.

"Do not lose faith. It will take a bit of practice. This is how you get her to move."

Lavina showed him how to urge the mare forward and without resistance, the horse started forward.

"You make it look so easy," he commented as they rode along. Lavina pointed out various family's farms, explaining their crafts while giving pointers for driving.

"I believe it is in my bloodline now," Lavina replied. She looked speculatively at Adam.

"Why have you decided to make such a drastic change in your life?"

Adam stared straight ahead without responding but Lavina saw a muscle twitch in his jawline.

"I apologize. I did not intend to upset you but I imagine I will not be the only person asking this question," she told him softly. "You need not answer me."

Adam seemed to relax but he did not look at her.

"Sometimes you just get a wake-up call and realize that everything you've ever known is not necessarily everything you've always needed. I don't know if that makes any sense to you."

It made perfect sense to Lavina and she almost laughed.

"What makes you believe that you will find the peace you are seeking here with us?"

Adam turned and faced her, an undecipherable expression on his face.

"I can't think of a time that I have felt more at peace than this minute," he replied and Lavina felt a slow blush rise into her cheeks.

They stopped outside of Millersburg and Lavina pointed to the quaint town.

"Our family's furniture shop is there," she told him. "I can show it to you another time."

"Why not now?" he asked and Lavina looked at him in surprise. She did not expect that he would be interested.

"Fine," she agreed and the continued on Railroad Street toward East Jackson Street. "May I ask what you did for a living in Toledo?"

"I was a financial advisor," he told her. Lavina found herself staring at him open-mouthed.

"Were you successful?"

"Very."

She stopped herself from asking any more questions despite her burning desire.

If he wants to tell me more, he will. But why would a rich man throw everything away to live so simply among the Amish? What does he see here that I do not?

"This is our family store," she told him as they pulled in front of the modest shop on North Grant Street. Adam leaned forward to peer into the store, his azure eyes shining with appreciation.

"Your people take so much pride in their work. There is such a sense of honor and family in your community. It is not like that with us."

Not all of them, Lavina thought sourly, thinking of Eli and his philandering ways. *There are unscrupulous people everywhere.*

Immediately, Lavina wondered what was wrong with her. She was in the company of a charming, appreciative man and her mind was wandering toward a serpent in the grass.

You should enjoy your time with this man while you are still here, she told herself.

They drove around town a while longer before heading back toward the district.

"Will I see you again tomorrow?" Adam asked hopefully and Lavina nodded.

"Tomorrow we will practice our Pennsylvania German. How much do you know?"

Adam gave her a look which told her she had much work to accomplish.

I will have to simply speak only to him in our language so he learns, Lavina decided.

Driving away from the Umble farm, Lavina found herself glancing over her shoulder to see if he was watching after her. He was.

The days began to pass at rapid speed and suddenly, two weeks had gone by. Adam had proven to be a model student and their time had begun to sway Lavina's thoughts of leaving.

Instead, she found herself more consumed with wanting to hold his hand and maybe steal a kiss.

Once he is baptized, he will be regarded as a member of this community just as anyone else. Perhaps we will have a future together, Lavina thought one evening, staring dreamily out the window as she did the supper dishes.

"Who is that Englisher you are always with?"

Lavina dropped the plate in her hand and whirled to confront the man who had crept into the kitchen. She glanced around but he family had retired to the front room and were out of earshot.

"Eli, do you not know how to use the front door?" she demanded, furiously. She bent down to pick up the broken dish at her feet.

"I asked you a question," he demanded, advancing on her. Lavina sprung to her feet and glared at him.

"You have no right to ask me anything. Get out of here before I call for my father, Eli!" she snapped but her heart was racing. His hazel eyes narrowed dangerously.

"You cannot walk out of my life that simply, Lavina. We are going to be married."

Lavina snorted and parted her lips to call for Elmo but to her relief, Eli stepped back and put his hand on the doorknob.

"You should really reconsider how you are treating me, Lavina."

He was gone before she could respond and Lavina sank against the sink, her heart pounding furiously in her chest.

Lavina raced to the top of the stairs where her sisters were already gathered.

"What is going on?" she hissed and they shushed her in unison. She crouched down to watch the scene at the front door where her father was speaking to another elder.

"...he refuses to repent. He is just sitting there smirking like a petulant child."

"I do not care about that right now," Elmo growled in a low tone, glancing back up at the stairwell. From his position, he could not see his daughters but he could likely sense them. When someone came knocking at three o'clock in the morning, it was apt to wake up the entire household.

"Where is the boy?"

The neighbor sighed and shook his head.

"He was taken by ambulance to Joel Pomerene Memorial Hospital. It was awful. So much blood..."

Elmo reached for his hat and coat, shaking his head.

"What happened?" Lavina demanded again. "Who got hurt."

Simultaneously, the three women turned to stare sympathetically at her.

"Lavina, Eli Smucker went to the Umble's home and beat Adam Everly with a wrought iron pipe," Elizabeth whispered.

Lavina screamed.

"*Daed,* go faster, please!" Lavina begged as they plodded toward the hospital in Millersburg.

"It does not matter how fast we go, Lavina. They will not allow for us to see him when we arrive," Elmo replied gently. The thought that she would not see Adam filled her with panic.

"Why not? Someone needs to be there for him!"

"If he is not in intensive care, we will see him when visiting hours start."

Intensive care? How badly did Eli hurt him? He is a madman! How can someone do something like that to another human being?

"Adam will never stay now," she breathed, the realization bringing about a sweeping bout of nausea.

"He will," Elmo assured her.

"How can you believe that? He came here because he thought people were different here. Now he will see that we have just as much evil and corruption as anywhere else."

"No Lavina, he came here because he was dying," Elmo replied quietly. Lavina's head whipped around so fast, she was shocked it did not fly completely off her shoulders.

"What do you mean he was dying?" she choked.

Elmo sighed and out of the corner of her eye, Lavina could see a sprinkling of lights from the town.

"Adam was diagnosed with stage four stomach cancer last year. Like many people who are facing death, he began to wonder why he had worked so hard without enjoying his life. He looked around at his expensive apartment and his fancy shoes and he realized that he wanted none of it. He wanted to live and live simply without the weight of the world upon his shoulders."

"But, Daed, he is never sick! He wakes at dawn and works all day. You cannot be right!"

"He won the battle against the cancer and he is in remission but it could return any time as cancer does. Adam vowed that he would not fall into the same trap which had run his life. He was sure that if he continued to live as he had, the cancer would return. Adam blamed his lifestyle for his poor health."

Lavina paused to register what her father had said, her mind spinning in dozens of directions.

"Is that why he put the time restriction on himself? He was worried that the cancer might return and he would not be accepted to join the church if he was sick?"

"We would never have turned him away for being sick, Lavina. In fact, we allowed for him to come into our fold because we were moved by his dedication to renouncing the outside world and accepting God's will. But yes, he wanted to ensure he was not brought in by pity but by virtue of earning his place."

Elmo stopped speaking and turned to Lavina, his eyes shiny against the black night.

"This is also why I asked you to teach him our ways," Elmo continued.

"Why?" Lavina was confused, her soul heavy with emotion.

"You have been questioning your path also. I know you have been ready to leave us since that boy broke your heart."

She was shocked by the revelation.

"How did you -?"

"Lavina, you forget that not only am I a minister in our district, I am also the father who loves you without end. When my children hurt, I become terminal. I found out the day after that girl showed up at worship. I cannot say I was upset at the time; I did not think of Eli as a good match for you but that was not my place to speak."

Lavina stared at him in awe. Any other father she knew would certainly have made it a point to object to the match but her father wanted her to learn from her own mistakes.

"I also knew that his true character would rear its ugly head and you would see him for the charming snake he is. You have always been a smart girl, Lavina."

He set me up to spend time with Adam so I would remember the goodness of living in this community. He hoped I would reconsider my actions before I did anything I would regret. He was right.

"Daed," Lavina asked tearfully as they drew near the hospital. "Is he going to die?"

"No, Lavvy. I believe Jacob Umble wrestled off Eli before too much damage was done. He was conscious when they took him and asking for you apparently."

Lavina's brown eyes were overflowing with tears.

He was asking for me.

His face was swollen with bruising and Lavina almost did not recognize him as she rushed into the room. She and her father had been in the waiting area since five o'clock in the morning and Lavina was a bundle of nerves.

"You may see Mr. Everly now, Miss Blauch, Mr. Blauch," the bored nurse intoned at eight o'clock. Lavina sprung to her feet but Elmo remained seated.

"Are you not coming?" she asked when she realized her father was not on her heels.

"I will go after you see him," he told her encouragingly. Lavina offered him a thankful smile.

"Danke, Dat," she whispered. He nodded.

"Oh!" Lavina gasped as Adam turned to face her. His eyes were red balls of puffiness and she could not see the vivid blue of his eyes.

"It looks worse than it is," he joked, his voice coming out in short rasps. Lavina swallowed the lump in her throat and hurried toward him.

"What did the doctor say?"

"He said I will heal and that next time I should try to fight back. I told him that I haven't done any training in REM sleep martial arts but I will consider it."

Lavina did not smile, a flash of fury toward Eli stabbing through her.

What a tough man, attacking someone when they are asleep.

She pushed Eli out of her mind and leaned forward to caress his battered face.

"When will you get out?" she asked, her hands shaking.

"They want to keep me one more night just to be sure but I'll be back tomorrow."

"What will you need? I will come to the Umble's every day and take care of you until you are well again."

Adam smiled weakly.

"Well, the doctor did say I needed one thing but it's big so I don't know – "

"Anything!" Lavina replied quickly. "What is it?"

Adam's hand reached up to enfold hers.

"He told me I needed the love of a woman named Lavina Blauch."

Lavina began to sob and she lowered her head against his chest.

"You already have that," she bawled. "I am not going anywhere."

AMISH GIRL IN THE BIG APPLE

ABBY BARKER

It had taken months of begging and pleading to Mama and Papa, but they finally gave in. Ever since she was a little girl, Abby had an obsession with New York City. There was something about its bustling streets, towering buildings, and even its grit and grime that was so opposite to her small Amish community out in the countryside that unrelentingly called out to her. Each time her family passed through neighboring towns on their way to some market or trade show, she'd soak up every billboard and image depicting the towering skyline of the city that never sleeps.

Abby's parents always thought of her fascination with the city as a passing phase, something all young girls go through in some form or another, but once she turned sixteen she began talking more seriously about leaving home. Mama and Papa went away on rumspringa themselves when they were around her age, but they were still nervous thinking about their only daughter running off to the big city. At first, they insisted she pick a smaller, less intimidating city to visit, like Philadelphia or even Chicago where they had family that could keep on eye on her, but Abby was relentless. They tried to convince her to wait until her younger cousin was old enough to go with her to no avail. Abby had been waiting to go to New York City for as long as she could remember and once she turned eighteen she decided she couldn't wait a single second longer.

That morning, bags packed and dressed for travel, Abby sat down at the breakfast table and told her parents that she was leaving that day, with or without their permission. Not wanting to harbor any ill feelings toward their daughter or to explain to their neighbors that she ran off against their wishes, Mama and Papa gave in with a collective defeated sigh. Abby jumped up like a shot and hugged both her parents at once, almost knocking them to the floor.

"Thank you, thank you, thank you! I promise I'll be okay. Sarah's cousin has an apartment in Manhattan and she said I could stay with her for as long as I want and you don't even have to worry about money because Sarah says everyone in New York serving food at restaurants and it would be super easy for me to get a job, even without any experience or anything. I'll write to you every day, or every other day, or when I have time. It's New York, after all. I'm going to have so much to do! It's all so exciting!"

Abby flashed her parents a bright, enthusiastic smile that they tried to replicate, but their nerves stood in the way. Sarah was Abby's best friend from school. Her parents never let her go on rumspringa because of her cousin, Grace. Grace left home to visit the city when she was eighteen and never came back. Sarah's family was devastated, but Sarah kept in touch with Grace and was assured that she was happy and had made the right choice. Sarah's parents didn't want to take the risk that she might do the same.

"Just...be careful. Remember what you have waiting for you back at home."

"Listen to your Mama. This will always be your home. God has a path set for you here."

Abby brushed off her parents' words of caution with a closed-lipped smile and a small shrug. She understood their concern, but a week, or month, or year in New York wouldn't change her fundamental beliefs, and if it did would that automatically be a bad thing? Grace has lived in New York and away from the church for five years now and she was still a good person. Why did being Amish mean she had to hide herself away from the rest of the world her whole life? If she didn't go see the city she's dreamed of her entire life now then she never would. Besides, she was pretty sure she'd come back home. Her parents shouldn't worry so much.

Mama and Papa insisted she stay for one last meal before she caught the bus one town over that said "New York City" on the front. Abby could barely sit still long enough to bring bites of food to her mouth without shaking them off her fork. She'd seen that bus come and go hundreds of times, but that was the day she'd be going with it. Her mother tried to keep up a normal conversation, but Abby could only respond with "yes" or "no." Her mind was officially elsewhere. Eventually her father excused her from the table and she almost ran right out the door, but a small pang in her stomach stopped her at the threshold. Abby was unquestionably excited to start her journey, but she realized that she would miss her parents along the way. She slowed down for a moment to hug them both goodbye.

"Mama, Papa, I love you both very much. I'll see you when I get back."

She added that last part mostly to reassure her parents, but also a little bit for herself. She'd always imagines what might happen if she decided to stay in New York. She'd work hard to become an actress on Broadway, and one night a handsome fan would come to her dressing room after a particularly stirring performance and confess his love for her. It would turn out that he came from a rich family, of course, and even though she could absolutely support herself being a successful actress and all, she'd be in love and carefree for the rest of her life in a Manhattan penthouse. That was all a harmless fantasy, but the walk to the bus stop was absolutely real. An ounce of nervousness mixed with the excitement swirling around in her head.

She made it just on time, walked on to the half-filled bus, handed her ticket to a stone-faced bus driver and found a seat by the window. She wanted to see every inch of the city as they drove into it. An older woman with a lap full of knitting sat next to her and smiled. The familiarity calmed her a bit. Her mother spent the weekends knitting one and purling two after the morning's chores were finished. It would be a few hours before the skyline even came into view and the slow rocking of the bus soon lulled Abby to sleep.

Two or three hours later, she wasn't sure exactly, a particularly large bump in the road jostled Abby awake. The woman next to her was still knitting what now looked like a child-sized sweater. A quick look out the window revealed the view she'd been dreaming of for eighteen years. Abby clutched the small backpack she brought packed full of all her possessions to her chest and gasped. It was exactly like the pictures, but it also wasn't. Nothing could have prepared her for the jagged line of towering buildings that rose up out of the ground in front of her. The old woman chuckled.

"First time in New York City, dear?"

"Is it that obvious? I've always wanted to visit, but this is the first time my parents actually let me on a bus."

"Well, I prefer the quiet of the country now, but I spent a fair amount of my younger years wandering through the city streets. My daughter lives in Manhattan, so when I visit I get live vicariously through her. I can never stay for too long, though. These old bones can't withstand the hustle and bustle like they used to. Stay out all night for me at least once, will you? There's nothing like Times Square once all the tourists have gone back to their hotels."

Abby tried to assure her that she was going to do everything in New York, especially Times Square, but the woman seemed to lose herself in the memory, smiling down at the knitting in her lap. Abby didn't mind the sudden end to their conversation, it only assured her that sometimes just thinking about being in New York City was better than whatever you were actually doing. Her nails dug into the sides of her backpack as she tried to contain her excitement.

Sarah had given Grace all of Abby's bus information: bus number, time of departure and arrival, where it was going to drop her off. She promised to meet her there and help her figure out the subway.

"I can probably do it on my own. She don't have to go out of her way," Abby had said to Sarah, but Sarah said Grace had laughed kindly and told her there was no way she was going to let an Amish teenage girl get lost in New York on her very first day.

"She might end up wandering around Coney Island and I won't have that."

The streets started to narrow as the bus made it's way deeper into the city and closer to their destination. They passed small corner stores with yellow banners marked "Deli Grocery," and pop-up street vendors selling flowers or fruit or both. Abby tried to remember the face of every new person she saw. Everyone was so different here than in her homogeneous Amish community back home and she loved it. Each unique face had a different story behind it. What did the woman without shoes dressed all in tie-dye do all day? What about the old man in a crisp, tailored suit who read a book while he walked? She loved this city and she hadn't even stepped off the bus yet.

At the bus stop, she recognized Grace right away. Not only could she have been Sarah's somehow older twin, but she was also holding a big poster board sign that said, "Welcome to the Big Apple, Little Amish Girl!" Grace must have recognized her, too, because the moment Abby stepped off the bus she sprinted over and wrapped her in a huge hug, dropping the poster into the street.

"You're finally here! Welcome, welcome, welcome! I'm so excited to have someone from back home come visit me. I love it here, but there's something comfortable about that little town, huh? You excited? You ready for your stay at Casa de Grace?"

Abby knew Grace was kind and outgoing from Sarah's descriptions of her, but she had no idea how energetic she was. Going from the quiet, slow-talking lifestyle back home to Grace's immediate exuberance matched only by the city's chatter behind her was a little overwhelming for her. She could only manage an enthusiastic smile and nod while stumbling over the words, "Yes, okay, I'm ready!" Grace released her from the hug, picked up her sign with one hand, and locked hands with Abby with the other. Abby watched Grace's free-flowing curly hair bounce along behind her as she chatted about everything she wanted to do together while Abby was here. She had dyed it red and let it loose after moving to the city, and Abby admired it. Her dusty blonde locks were almost always pinned tightly to the back of her head and hidden under a bonnet. She left the bonnet at home this time, but the pins remained. She wondered if Grace would help her dye her own hair, maybe black, or blue even. Her parents would love that.

Grace excitedly rattled on about Strawberry Fields in Central Park, and eventually making it to the Statue of Liberty because she hasn't been there in ages, and of course they had to see a Broadway show, there were supposed to be a couple good ones premiering soon, never letting go of Abby's hand. A couple of blocks later, they descended into a subway station and stopped at an automated kiosk to purchase a MetroCard. Abby had never interacted with a machine this complex before and almost froze, not quite knowing what to do with the ball of crumpled bills in her hand. Luckily, Grace was quick to remember what life back home was like and thoughtfully helped her through the process. Holding the bright yellow and blue card in her hand made her feel very grown up and independent. She even made it through the turnstile on the first try.

"You're a natural, Abby! You were made for New York," exclaimed Abby.

Maybe I am, Abby thought.

Mama and Papa may have had more to worry about than a daughter with blue hair.

Grace took a break from listing every attraction in New York City to look down at her cell phone as they took their seats. Abby wrapped her arms tightly around the backpack on her lap and looked around the half-filled car. The subway was a completely new experience for her. She had never been on a bus before, either, but she had seen buses and the types of people on them. *This is like, an underground bus,* she told herself, not completely comfortable with being so far beneath the earth. She focused on the other people sharing the car. Just like the people on the street, no two of them were exactly the same. A tattooed mother sat quietly bouncing a child in her lap, while a teen a few seats down mirrored that image with a boom box blaring hip-hop.

Abby jumped as the train began to move. Grace chuckled and put a hand on her arm.

"I did the same thing on my first subway ride. Turned out I was on the right train but headed the wrong way so I had bigger fish to fry than dealing with being on a train for the first time," she threw back her head and laughed at the memory. "Once I realized I was no where near where I wanted to be I got off the train and started asking people which train would take me where I needed to be and they just kept telling me the one I was on. I didn't realize that the train going in the right direction was just on the other side of the platform. Man, did I feel dumb, but you won't have to worry about that, you have me!"

The two girls chatted for a little while as the train made it's way to their stop. Once they emerged back onto the city streets Abby began to get a feel for the constant flow of people. She quickened her pace to match Grace's and only bumped shoulders with a handful of people as she weaved through the crowd. Eventually, they walked into a tall building where a man sat at a desk by the door.

"Morning, Fred! This is my, well, she's basically my cousin. Abby's gonna be staying with me for a while so don't surprised if she comes flying through here at all hours of the day, okay?"

"Not a problem, Gracie! A friend of yours is a friend of mine. Nice to meet you, Abby!"

Abby smiled and waved at him as they walked to the elevator. She was surprised at how friendly everyone seemed to be. On the odd occasion that she did get her parents to talk with her about New York all they had to say about it was how unwholesome and rude the people were. She'd have to tell them how wrong they were when she got back. *If* she went back.

"That's my doorman, Fred. He's awesome. Always happy to see you even in the middle of the night. If you get yourself locked out or something and I'm not around Fred will help you out."

"That's good to know, thanks. Is everyone in New York this friendly?"

Grace laughed again.

"Not at all. Don't get me wrong, you'll find friendly people if you look for them but a lot of people would run you over with their cars and never look back. They're not bad people, they just have things to do and places to be and no time to stop and check if you're alive or not. That's your problem."

Grace saw a look of dismay cross over Abby's face.

"Don't worry, though. I'll make sure to introduce you to all the best people in New York. You just make sure not to get hit by any cars."

The elevator dinged as they made it to the fourteenth floor. Grace's apartment was at the end of the hall. It had two bedrooms, both with views overlooking the busy streets below, a small kitchen, a bathroom to share, and a living room filled with paintings and posters and a million other colorful decorations. Abby noticed a picture of Grace and Sarah from years ago sitting on a table by the couch. Before she could walk over to get a better look, Grace waved her into one of the two bedrooms. The room had a few pieces of art on the walls, but wasn't near as covered as the living room. A small bed was pushed up against the wall and dresser sat across from it with a TV placed on top.

"This is your room! I moved a bunch of stuff out of it and into the living room so you wouldn't be overwhelmed. I've only been here for a couple of years but I've managed to collect so much junk. I guess that's what happens when you go from a simple Amish life on the family farm to the big city. I can show you how to use the TV, too. I wouldn't blame you if you spent your first couple of days here just sitting in front of it watching cartoons. I know I did."

It was tempting, but Abby had been waiting to be a part of this city for so long she almost felt cooped up just being in the room to drop her things off.

"I'll definitely watch some TV later, but right now all I want is to explore or maybe find I job. I promised my parents I wouldn't ask them for money."

"Oh! I forgot to tell you. I know the manager of the diner down the street. He said he was looking for waitresses so I told him about you. He wants you to come down tomorrow morning so he can make sure you're not a total klutz or anything but you've basically got the job! How do you feel about pancakes?"

"I love pancakes! Thank you so much, Grace. You've done too much already."

"Don't even worry about it. I know what it's like being cooped up on a farm with no electricity or entertainment or fun. I want to make sure you're trip is the complete opposite of that! All fun, all the time. So, what do you want to do first?"

They spent the rest of the day just walking around Manhattan. They stopped for coffee at a sidewalk café, bought a few outfits fit for work at a department store, watched the dogs run around at the dog park. It was a fairly average day in New York but to Abby it was the best day of her life. Grace was a wealth of information, only stopping the flow to take sips of her latte. She knew the best place to get a burger, the best place for live music, the best cup of coffee – this wasn't it, but it would do.

"It's almost dinner time so why don't we start with the best Chinese takeout and spend the evening just hanging out at my place. How does that sound? You must be exhausted!"

She was exhausted, but she'd never admit it. She could only agree that Chinese food did sound good, even though she'd never had it before, and she wouldn't mind a night in. They stopped at a hole-in-the-wall restaurant only distinguishable by its vaguely oriental décor. Grace never once looked at the menu as she rattled off a list of food: crab rangoons, fried rice, sweet and sour chicken, lo mien, and don't forget the fortune cookies! When they got back to the apartment, Grace spread the feast out on her coffee table, handed Abby a pair of chopsticks, and said "Dig in!" After some fumbling with the sticks, she was able to shovel mountains of delicious and greasy food into your mouth.

While they watched the movie "Mean Girls," one of Grace's favorites, Abby broke open a fortune cookie. One side listed a handful of lucky numbers and the other said, "A big surprise is coming your way." She had spent so much time planning for this trip, accounting for every little detail, she wondered what surprises the city could possibly have in store for her. She could hardly sleep that night thinking about it. Maybe she wouldn't get the job. Maybe New York wouldn't live up to her expectations, but that couldn't be it because they already had. Maybe it would be something else, something so surprising that she couldn't even imagine it yet. She hoped that was it.

***

In the morning, Grace woke Abby up with a gentle shake and a steaming cup of coffee.

"Morning sunshine! It's your first day of work and I don't want you to be late. Here, I made you some coffee and I picked out an outfit for you last night, but you don't have to wear it. Sorry I'm acting like such a mom after you came all this way to get away from your parents. Yikes!"

Abby laughed, "I wasn't running *away* from my parents, I was running *to* New York! Thank you for the pleasant wakeup call."

"Well, I was definitely running from my parents. Living in that house was stifling; all those rules, no fun, and for what? God's plan? Sorry, I just get a little frustrated sometimes thinking about all the things my parents kept from me back home. I still feel religious from time to time, but the rigid rules of Amish life just aren't for me."

"Yeah, I know what you mean. I feel like there's so much I want to do that I just can't there. That's why I wanted to come here. I want to get it all out of my system so that I can go back to living simply. Once I've done everything I'll probably be so exhausted that I'll want to go back anyways!"

Grace smiled at her kindly, but bit her tongue. She knew better than most that it didn't always work that way. She didn't want to influence Abby's choice either way, but life as she saw it couldn't just be flushed out of someone's system. A person either craves an Amish life, or an English one. Abby just had to decide which it was she wanted most.

"We can talk about the serious stuff later. Why don't you jump in the shower and get ready for work while I cook breakfast. Go ahead and use whatever you find in there. Mi shampoo es tu shampoo!"

Abby washed herself, changed into the clothes Grace picked out for her, and played around with her makeup. Back home she didn't have any of this stuff. You didn't need makeup to go to church. Plus, every boy she knew had known her since they were children. They'd just be confused if she showed up to the Sunday sing one day covered in powders and creams, but here, no one knew her. She could wear as much or as little makeup as she wanted and no one would question it. Abby decided to start small, only applying a small amount of blush and a couple coats of mascara. The thick frame of lashes made her eyes look huge and the soft pink on her cheeks gave her the appearance of being a little bit warm. Even this small amount of makeup looked jarring in the mirror, but she also kind of liked it.

When she finally emerged from the bathroom Grace was dancing around her kitchen using a spatula as a microphone. At the end of an exaggerated spin she saw Abby standing in the hall giggling.

"Hey! You look awesome! You even threw on some makeup? That's advance level stuff. Now you just need to learn to flirt a little bit and you'll be swimming in tips."

"I know how to flirt!" Abby said defensively.

"Ha! Staring at a boy across the room during prayer is not flirting. New York's a completely different world."

"Oh yeah? How different can city boys be?"

"You know what? You might be right. All you have to do is blink those big doe eyes at one of these too-cool-for-school guys and they'll be smitten. You'll do fine."

"I don't even know if I want to date anyways."

"Oh, you'll change your mind the first time a cute boy tells you he likes your smile. Trust me. It happens to the best of us."

They talked a little bit about boys and back home over breakfast before it was time for Abby to head to the diner. It was so close to Grace's apartment building that she brought Abby down to the lobby, pointed to the place on the corner, sent her on her way and told her to ask for a man named Greg. She was a little nervous to go on her own, but this was exactly the experience that she was hoping to have in New York. Abby craved a taste of independence and she was finally getting it.

The diner was called "Rizzo's Place" and it looked exactly how she'd pictured a classic New York diner. The tables and chairs were all covered in turquoise vinyl complete with little flecks of glitter and the wait staff were all wearing crisp white aprons and matching paper hats. The aprons reminded her of her mother's back home, but that was the only ounce of familiarity she felt. The restaurant was fairly busy. Early morning was their rush hour, but that had passed so only a handful of stragglers and early lunch-eaters remained. She was standing by the doorway when a man only a little older than her wandered over to see if she wanted a table.

"Hey there! Can I help you?"

"I'm looking for Greg. I'm supposed to start working today."

The man's face broke out into a huge smile and he leaned in for a hug.

"You must be Abby! Grace told me all about you and how hardworking and great you are. Grace and I are like this," he crossed his fingers to show that they were close, "so I'd do anything for that girl. Oh! I'm Greg by the way."

Abby gathered from his tone that he might be gay. She had met one gay boy before back in her town, but he hadn't told anyone aside from her and a few friends about his sexuality. It wasn't something that bothered her, but seeing a man so openly flamboyant surprised and encouraged her. She had always thought of New York as a place where everyone could be exactly who they wanted to be, and seeing this man live up to that ideal was exciting. Abby smiled back and nodded.

"That's me! Thank you so much for giving me this job."

"You're so cute! Abby, you're going to fit in just fine here. I almost don't even think I have to train you. Want to just throw on an apron and dive right in?"

When a nervous look crossed over Abby's face he added, "All you have to do first is introduce yourself and ask if they'd like anything to drink. They usually just want coffee or water. If they want coffee make sure to ask about cream and sugar. I'll only give you one table for now so don't worry! If you flop, I'll be here to help you out but you seem like a natural!"

Greg scoped the restaurant to see which table he wanted to throw at her.

"Okay, there's one guy sitting in the corner. He's a regular. He usually just comes in for a coffee, sometimes scrambled eggs with a side of bacon, but nothing too complicated. Nice guy. Are you ready?"

Abby nodded. Greg smiled and gently pushed her forward. She didn't realize how quickly she'd be thrown into the actual serving part of the job, but she wasn't about to embarrass herself so she threw back her shoulders and approached the table as confidently as she could.

"Hey there! I'm Abby. Can I get you a coffee to drink? I mean, can I get you anything?"

From far away she couldn't tell how subtly attractive the man in the booth was. He was partially hidden by a beanie hat and an oversize sweatshirt, but when she got closer Abby could see a sharp jaw line and kind eyes beneath the baggy outerwear. She was thrown off by her attraction for a moment, but her desire to impress her new boss prevailed. She flashed him a professional smile as she bit her tongue.

"Yeah, sure, a black coffee would be great."

"Can I get you anything else?"

"Not right now, thanks."

She turned on her heal and walked back to Greg, not sure where she was supposed to take the order. Luckily, he was watching enthusiastically from the sidelines cheering her on silently.

"How'd it go? Was he nice? What am I saying, he's always nice! What did he order?'"

"Just a black coffee."

"Yep, that sounds like him. Let me show you where the coffee station is."

Greg helped her find the station and pour a cup. He showed her where the cream and sugar was, just in case her next customer needed it. He then showed her how to use the computer system in order to keep track of what each customer ordered. This was all very simple, however, and it wasn't long until she was right back at her only customer's table with the cup of coffee.

"Here you are, sir. One cup of black coffee."

"Thanks, but why are you talking like that. It sounds like you're a robot who was programmed to work in a diner."

Abby blushed.

"Oh, well it's my first day. Sorry. I'm still trying to get the hang of things."

The customer looked a little embarrassed as well. He didn't mean to call her out.

"No, I mean, I'm sorry. I didn't mean to embarrass you. Thanks for the coffee. It's great, as always."

Abby gave him a polite, but uncomfortable, half smile and turned to walk away but he stopped her.

"Wait, what's your name?"

"Abby."

"Abby, like Abigail?"

"No. Just Abby, actually. My mom just liked Abby."

"That's a nice name. Mine's Mac, like Mackenzie. My mom wanted a girl, but got me instead, so she picked a gender-neutral name. I don't mind it, though."

"I like Mac. There aren't a lot of guys where I'm from with names like that."

"Oh yeah? Where is it that you're from?"

"It's a little Amish town just outside of here, actually. I just got into the city yesterday."

"Yesterday? You need someone to show you around then."

Abby blushed again. She thought about what Grace said about flirting for tips, but this felt more genuine than that. This guy, Mac, didn't seem to care about tips.

"I'd like that."

"Great! Give me your phone number and I'll call you up sometime."

"Oh, I don't have a phone number. I don't have a phone."

"That's right. The whole 'Amish' thing. Well, when do you get off here?"

Greg had been listening in the whole time and jumped into the conversation.

"Right now! She's done for the day, wasn't she amazing? I just have to teach her how to clock out and she'll be on her way!"

Greg pulled Abby to the side to chat, but Abby was confused.

"Did I do something wrong? Do you not want me to work here?"

"No! No, of course not. I've just seen this guy come in day in, day out and, don't get me wrong he's one of the nicest customers we have which is why I'm doing this, but he's never once brought in a date or left with one. It's just so cute seeing you two together I can't resist! Go! Have a good time and come back tomorrow and we'll give you some real training. It was my mistake for giving you the cute, single guy as your first table."

Abby almost didn't know what to do. She expected to start her first job, but instead she was going on her first date. She walked back over to Mac's table, Greg casually waving his hands to encourage her.

"Sorry about that. It looks like I'm free now."

"Great! I can take you to work with me then."

Abby had no idea what this entailed but Greg gave her a thumbs up and she followed Mac out of the diner. They walked for a few blocks, casually chatting about their lives. Mac was very interested in Abby's Amish community and Abby was very interested in where Mac was taking her. If it hadn't been for Greg's insistence, she probably wouldn't have felt comfortable following a man she just met through New York City, but she couldn't resist. Eventually, he led them into a building and up a few flights of stairs. Greg pulled back a sliding iron door to reveal a colorful studio filled with paintings and sculptures.

"This is where I work, and live, I guess."

"You're an artist!" Abby exclaimed.

"I'd like to think so, but I've been in a rut lately. I haven't been able to create anything new. I don't want to sound cliché, but would you mind if I tried painting you? You haven't even taken off your work apron yet and your eyes are just so beautiful."

He didn't comment on her smile, but Grace's words still ran through her mind as this boy asked if she'd model for him. On one hand, she was weary, but on the other his sincerity penetrated through most else. She didn't feel as though he wanted anything from her except for her image so she agreed. Mac and Abby sat mostly still for the next couple of hours as Mac swept acrylics across a large canvas, capturing Abby in that moment. When the painting was finally done he turned it around and approached her.

"Alright, here it is. How do you like it?"

Abby looked at herself, carefully depicted in paint. Mac had noticed her mascara covered eyes, but hadn't painted them in a cartoonish way. He'd only enhanced the features on her face that had already been beautiful.

"It's...gorgeous! Is that conceded to say?"

"No, not when you look like you do."

Mac leaned towards Abby to kiss her. She almost turned away, but her instincts took over. With his mouth on hers she finally felt free of her parents grasp and also just free in general. He pulled away before she was finished enjoying the moment.

"I don't want to overstep my boundaries here. I like you a lot, but where from two different worlds."

Abby smiled confidently for the first time and touched his face.

"This is exactly what I want," she said before leaning back in to finish the kiss.

***

The two teens dated for a few weeks after that first studio session. Abby posed for multiple paintings, some more revealing than others, but always with her expressed consent. She loved having her freedom. She loved being able to come and go from Grace's apartment as she wished, but eventually she got bored. One night, as Mac painted Abby holding a bouquet of roses while sitting on a couch, she finally hit her breaking point. She threw the roses up into the air and started to shout.

"Mac! I can't do this anymore. What's the point of me coming here, day after day, just to be your model?"

"You're gorgeous, Abby. You're my muse!"

"But what am I getting out of this? Where does this take me?"

Mac couldn't answer that and Abby got up to leave.

"This has been fun, Mac, but I don't have a purpose here. I think I need to go home."

Mac tried to convince her to stay. He tried to convince her that her portraits meant more to him than just simple trinkets, but she wasn't swayed. As fun as the city was, as much freedom as she had, home would always be back in her little farm town. God had always had a path laid out for her, and this turned out to be only a detour.